Mally Cox-Chapman

Baggywrinkle

illustrations by Sue Cartwright

D0892762

Scholastic Publications Ltd, London

First published 1977 by William Heinemann Ltd
This edition published for Scholastic Publications Ltd,
161 Fulham Road, London SW3 6SW 1979 by
Pan Books Ltd, Cavaye Place, London SW10 9PG
in association with William Heinemann Ltd
© Mally Cox-Chapman 1977
ISBN 0 330 25733 1
Made and printed in Great Britain by
C. Nicholls & Company Ltd, The Philips Park Press, Manchester

This book is for

Slade and Rachel for whom
the characters first came alive

Nicola, Richard, and Anita
who cheered them on their way

and most of all, to Jim
who believed in me
even when I did not.

Contents

A few words about magic 5

1 How Baggywrinkle was carved from a mast 6

2 The arrival of Timbuctoo 13

3 The journey begins and Timbuctoo causes some trouble 22

4 Trouble at the border 32

5 Out of the soup, into the cauldron 41

6 Meeting with the Mad Tycoon 49

7 To the dungeons 58

8 In search of spiders' webs 65

9 To the Sun 73

10 The very inside of the Sun 79

11 The plot thickens and boils 92

12 Why Baggywrinkle leaves his friends behind 99

13 The River of See-Through Things 103

Epilogue 111

A few words about magic

There is still some magic left in the world. Not as much as there used to be, since there are people who have been waging war against magic for years. But they haven't won yet. If you are quiet, and clever, and know where to look (like underneath tin cans, and near trees, or in attics) very often some magic is hidden there.

For instance, on the Ivory Coast of Africa, magic spirits live in the enormous Iroko trees. Most spirits live perfectly happily until they die of old age. But sometimes men come into the woods to cut down an Iroko tree and take it to the lumberyards where they build ships. When that happens, most tree-spirits die of heartbreak.

But one tree-spirit did not die of heartbreak. As they stripped off his bark and polished his wood he became more and more curious about what might happen next. By the time he was the smallest mast on a very large sailing schooner, he was practically popping with excitement. As well he should have been, because someday that spirit would be carved into a boy, which is what this story is about.

1 How Baggywrinkle was carved from a mast

All sorts of curious junk bobbed about in the water when the storm ended over the ocean. Most of the most curious junk came from a pirate ship that split in two when a monstrous wave hit it. This was inconvenient for the pirates, who all died immediately, but it was the beginning of an adventure for the ship's littlest mast, which broke off at its base and hurtled into the waves like a toothpick.

It was not very long before the mast floated on to a beach on the Ivory Coast of Africa, where it stayed for several days while the sun dried it through and through and turned it a most beautiful golden brown. On the fourth day, the mast heard the squish, squash, squish of someone's footsteps in the sand. The tree-spirit in the mast felt it might burst with loneliness. This was horrible, to be passed by silently after all those months listening to the songs and stories of the pirates. So, to its own surprise (since it had never tried before) the tree-spirit talked.

'Hey you. Don't go! Talk to me!'

The old man – for that's who the footsteps belonged to – stopped in his tracks. He looked all around, but there was no one in sight. So he scratched his head and shrugged his shoulders and started off again.

'Let me out of here,' repeated the tree-spirit's voice. 'I'm here. In the mast. I need your help.'

'Why, bless my pyjama bottoms,' said the old man. 'How did you get in there?'

'I've always been in here,' said the tree-spirit, 'but I didn't know I could talk until a few moments ago. There might be all sorts of things I could do if I didn't have to stay in this mast. Can you get me out?'

The old man was wise enough to see that the only way to get him out was by carving. And since his only friend was far away, it would be nice to have someone to talk to. So he rolled the mast home (for it was much too heavy for an old man with creaking joints to carry) and pushed it into his cottage. It was a small cottage made from the leaves of a palm tree, and filled with treasures from the ocean – bottles with boats in them, bottles with bits of coloured sea-glass, a set of toy soldiers, a grandfather clock that didn't work, and even a big brass bed.

It wasn't just by chance that there were so many wonderful things. Every morning, after the old man finished his breakfast of fried hibiscus flowers and bananas in milk, he'd take his walking stick and set out down the beach looking for treasures. So when the tree-spirit asked the old man's name, the old man smiled and said he was the Beachcomber, because he loved to comb the beaches.

After the Beachcomber had a cup of tea to settle his nerves (for even if you are a wise old man and know that there is magic left in the world, it still seems remarkable to hear a mast talk) he set to work chipping away at the mast with chisels and mallets and all the tools a sculptor might use. He had to be very careful, for one wrong cut and he might break off the nose or put a dent in the toes or chip off an inch from the middle. So the Beachcomber worked very slowly, tracing with his fingers along the grain of the wood to feel where the shapes wanted to emerge.

'How old are you?' he asked the tree-spirit.

'What do you mean, old?'

'How many years have you been alive?' said the old man. 'Should I carve you five years old, or twenty-five, or one hundred and five?'

'I only know I'm 1,632 rainstorms old,' said the tree-spirit.

'And I'm twenty-five thousand bananas-for-breakfast old,'

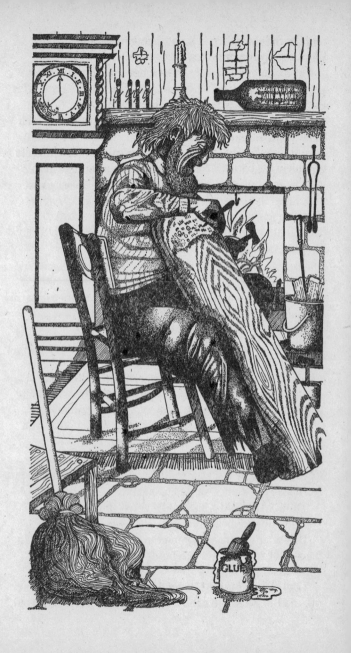

said the Beachcomber. 'Except that we usually measure age by years. How many years have you been alive?'

The spirit didn't exactly know what a year was, but he seemed to remember that he came into Being very soon after the Great Eclipse of the Sun. So the Beachcomber rummaged around his cottage for something that might tell them when that eclipse occurred.

'Hah!' exclaimed the old man, practically hidden in a pile of junk in the corner. '*Here* is my fireman's hat. I've been looking for that. And here's my green umbrella with holes in it. Hah! I've found it. *The Complete Astrological and Astronomical Almanac of the Universe.*' He thumbed through the pages. 'Well, you're either twelve years old or a hundred and forty. What'll it be, my friend?'

'Twelve!' And twelve years old he was.

So the old man got back to work and the two friends spent the afternoon talking and telling stories and deciding the length of a twelve-year-old nose, and twelve-year-old arms and twelve-year-old legs.

Anyone looking into the cottage who didn't know what was going on might have thought it was pretty weird. Picture an old man, even older than your grandfather, sitting in front of the fireplace in a small cottage by the edge of the sea. He had shaggy white hair all over his head, and lots of white whiskers too. His trousers are too big for him and his sweater is too small. There he is all by himself, talking and laughing and telling stories as he sandpapers away at the golden piece of wood in front of him. If the outsider didn't walk away feeling just a little frightened of a jabbering old man talking to himself, he would hear, 'Hey Beachcomber, when am I going to be done? Can't you hurry up?'

Then the old man smiles and says, 'Patience, my friend, patience, that is what the sea teaches.'

When all the carving and sandpapering were done, the

Beachcomber polished the golden brown wood until it was almost as smooth as skin. Then he rubbed the wood with lemon oil until it was sleek, and the joints moved easily and without a squeak.

But the Beachcomber didn't know what to give him for hair. 'Would you mind terribly being bald?'

'Mind being bald! You bet I do! Whoever heard of a bald twelve-year-old?'

So the Beachcomber poked around his cottage to see what he could find. There was some milkweed fluff, but it was white and tended to float away. An old mop sat underneath the piano seat, but the Beachcomber sneezed every time he got near it. Finally he found a clump of frayed rope that had washed up on shore just a few days before. Since it was fuzzy and curly, the old man took the golden brown stuff and, with paste made from a periwinkle shell, glued it to the wooden head.

No sooner were the final strands glued on when the Someone began to move. He sat up on the table and brushed off all the sawdust. He tested all his moving parts. He wriggled his ears, and bent at the knees, and waved his hands.

'I'm a boy,' he said with wonder in his voice. 'I'm an ordinary twelve-year-old, just-like-everybody-else boy! I'm the right size, and I've got legs and arms and toes, and I can even feel my heart pounding. How did it happen, Beachcomber? I'm not a mast any more! I'M A BOY!'

The Beachcomber was so happy he just stood there for a moment scratching his head in amazement. He could hardly talk in complete sentences. 'I don't know what to say. It's like a miracle,' said the old man at last. 'It must be magic.'

The boy put his hands to his head and felt his fuzzy hair. 'All of a sudden I felt this rush of warmth, like summer wind, as you were putting on my hair. It's just like that stuff sailors put on the ropes of big boats. You know, it's called … um …'

'Why, of course, it's Baggywrinkle!' said the Beachcomber.

'Baggywrinkle!' said the boy. He jumped off the table and began to sing:

I'm as dashing and brave as can be,
My friend will tell you the same.
I'm now in the world to see what's to see,
Baggywrinkle is my name.

Never before did I know that I could
Be more than a mast at sea.
But I talk and I walk, though once I was of wood.
Banana hosanna! It's me!

You should have seen the Beachcomber as his wrinkly old face crinkled into a smile. A friend to talk to. And take walks with, and share his treasures with. And the friend could sing, too! In a burst of energy he took Baggywrinkle's hands and started to dance a jig. But Baggywrinkle stumbled, and then he fell flat on his face. And when he picked himself up, he bumped smack into the Beachcomber.

'Are you all right?' asked the Beachcomber. 'Can't you see where you're going? Baggywrinkle, quick, tell me how many fingers I'm holding up.'

'I don't know,' said Baggywrinkle. 'I can't see, for some reason.' He rubbed his eyes.

The Beachcomber flung open the window. 'Well then, what colour is the sky today?' he demanded, trying to hide the fear in his voice.

'I don't know,' said Baggywrinkle.

The Beachcomber took the boy by the hand and led him out to the beach. 'Now,' said the Beachcomber, 'what colour is the ocean? Blue or green?'

'I don't *know*,' said Baggywrinkle frantically. 'I can hear the waves swoosh. I can smell the seaweed drying in the sun. But ... I ... oh Beachcomber, I can't tell you the colour of

11

the ocean. What has happened? I used to be able to see. I saw you, didn't I? What's happened, Beachcomber?'

The Beachcomber's shoulders sagged. 'I've made a mistake,' he said. 'A terrible, awful mistake. I must have made you blind.'

'Oh,' said Baggywrinkle. His voice quivered with fear. 'Does that mean we can't be friends?'

'No, no. Of course not,' said the Beachcomber. 'It just means I shall have to be your eyes for you. I carved your eyes so carefully. Why didn't the magic work for them? I suppose eyesight is too special to be carved. Oh, I don't know, I don't know.'

With all his heart Baggywrinkle wanted his eyesight. But that seemed so impossible that he ached all over and he could feel the tears coming. So while the Beachcomber put his arm around him to comfort him, Baggywrinkle cried and cried and cried. Finally he fell asleep. The Beachcomber carried him gently to the hammock on the porch of the cottage, and covered him with a blanket. For a while the old man just stood over the boy and rocked the hammock back and forth as he thought.

2 The arrival of Timbuctoo

The Beachcomber sat on the porch and watched over
Baggywrinkle, aching with sadness that Baggywrinkle was
blind. As the old man rocked back and forth in his rocking
chair he thought of all the things that Baggywrinkle would
not be able to do. He would not be able to explore by
himself – to find a tree that he specially loved, or discover a
secret hiding place, or peer at the sand after high tide for the
tiniest shells the sea sometimes leaves behind. And he
wouldn't be able to run up the hill in the evening to watch
the sun drop into the sea.

But as the stars came out, one by one, and the cool moist
evening air patted the old man's hands and face, the
Beachcomber realized that seeing wasn't the only way to
discover treasure. He would still be able to show
Baggywrinkle the smooth pearly touch on the inside curve
of the conch shell. He could teach Baggywrinkle the calls
of the seagulls when they warn that a storm is brewing in the
southwest. Baggywrinkle didn't need eyes for such
treasures.

Cheered by these thoughts, but still much too worried to
sleep, the Beachcomber reminded himself that
Baggywrinkle needed clothes. He lit the kerosene lamp
inside the cottage to hunt for materials. Soon he came out
on to the porch with the kerosene lamp in one hand and
scribbles and scrapples of junk in the other. Besides
scissors, needle and thread, he was holding half a canvas sail,
two blocks of wood left over from the mast, five strands of
leather, a large dull fish hook, a chisel and mallet, and an

old pair of red trousers that were ripped at both knees.

First he cut the red trousers into shorts and sewed up the holes in the pockets. For Baggywrinkle's belt, he braided three of the leather strands together, made a loop on one end with the fourth strand, and with the fifth attached the old fish hook to the other end. The old split sail was just big enough to make Baggywrinkle a sailor shirt and the old man added pockets from the scraps of the red trouser legs. Then, all night long and almost to dawn he carved two wooden shoes.

Just as dawn came, the Beachcomber saw a tiny speck against the pink sky. It came closer and closer until the old man recognized his friend, the beautiful bird called Timbuctoo. Timbuctoo is a World Traveller. She has flown to New Zealand. She has wintered in Borneo where walking fish breathe on land and skip over the mud. And she has spent some time at a boarding school in Switzerland where the only subjects studied are dreams and storytelling. She had been away for so many months, in fact, that the Beachcomber had given up hope of ever seeing her again. But here she was, landing on the arm of his rocking chair arranging her most beautiful feathers so that they shone in the sun.

'Timbuctoo!' whispered the Beachcomber joyfully. 'I've missed you so much! Where have you been?'

'Hello, old man,' replied Timbuctoo. 'I've been, well, everywhere. In fact, putting my natural modesty aside for a moment, I should say that I am the best travelled bird in the world. *And* the most beautiful. Don't you agree?'

The Beachcomber smiled fondly at his friend. She hadn't changed a bit.

'Where have you *been* all these months?' he said.

'Oh, time enough to explain all that,' said Timbuctoo. 'But who is *this*?'

'Baggywrinkle,' said the old man. 'He's my new friend. I

14

carved him from a mast, and he turned into a boy.'

'Must have been magic,' said Timbuctoo.

'But he's blind,' added the Beachcomber. 'I don't know why. He could see when he was a tree-spirit in the mast, but something happened. I don't understand it, Timbuctoo.'

'You're not supposed to understand magic,' said Timbuctoo impatiently. 'Listen to me a moment. You don't think that you can "see" the way *I* can see, do you?'

'Don't I?' asked the old man.

'Of course not,' said the beautiful bird. 'You can't "see" a storm coming, can you? You can't "see" a migration of delicious grasshoppers on the other side of the forest, can you?'

'But that's not seeing,' said the Beachcomber.

'It's not *your* kind of seeing.'

'Are you saying that he was able to "see" the way a tree-spirit sees, but now that he's a boy, Baggywrinkle has to learn to see the way a boy sees?' asked the Beachcomber.

'You are a wise old man,' said Timbuctoo. 'Why don't you just start breakfast, and leave the rest to me. What's his name, did you say?'

'Baggywrinkle,' said the old man as he picked up his walking stick. 'Wake him gently, Timbuctoo. He has been awfully sad.'

With that, the old man started towards the cottage, thoroughly cheered and looking forward to his breakfast. Meanwhile, Timbuctoo flew up on to Baggywrinkle's head. She nestled into his hair and whispered, 'Now, Baggywrinkle, try to remember your dream.'

What a wonderful dream he was having! It told him that he would go on a long voyage on a perfectly round ship to a river filled with things that are see-through, like honey and raindrops, windows and lemonade. Friends would help him in his travels, and he would sing for them. Most important, the dream told him that at the end of the river he would find his eyesight.

Have you ever noticed how the very best dreams are interrupted by your brother jumping up and down on your bed, or by your mother calling you to breakfast? Luckily for Baggywrinkle, Timbuctoo interrupted the dream of the River of See-Through Things at just the right moment. She had studied at the special school for dreams and storytelling in Switzerland.

Baggywrinkle woke with a start. 'What's going on?' he mumbled. He reached his hands up to his fuzzy hair. 'What's that sitting on my head?' he demanded in the fiercest voice he could.

It was Timbuctoo of course. She plopped down on Baggywrinkle's knee. 'I'm Timbuctoo, I am a World Traveller – and a friend of the Beachcomber's. I have feathers of every colour, more colours than you could believe. I'm going on a voyage with you.'

'B, bb, BU, BUT? But how did you know,' stammered Baggywrinkle, 'that I am going on a trip?'

'I felt it in my feathers,' she said. 'Come on, chum. Hop to. We have a lot of work to do.'

'But where are we going?' asked Baggywrinkle as he scrambled to his feet. 'I can't see anything.'

As he said that, Baggywrinkle suddenly felt very scared. Where was the Beachcomber? And what would he do if the Beachcomber had left him? 'Where's the Beachcomber?' he asked. Then, before she could answer, he called even louder, 'Beachcomber, help! Where are you?'

'Oh shush,' said Timbuctoo. 'He's just gone inside to make us some breakfast. Did you dream while you were asleep?'

'Dream? Why yes, I had a wonderful one,' said Baggywrinkle. 'It said I was going on a long voyage. First I had to find a perfectly round ship, and then I think I sailed on it to the River of See-Through Things. I had some friends with me and it was because of them I was going to be able to find my eyesight at the end of the River. But that's not true, is it?'

16

'Of course it's true,' said Timbuctoo. 'Dreams never lie.'

'You mean I'm going to go and find a River of See-Through Things just because of a dream?' asked Baggywrinkle. 'Why should I believe a dream?'

'Why not?' she replied. 'In any case, it's a chance for adventure. The Beachcomber and I will help you find your eyesight. To do that, we shall go on a quest together and have lots of adventures. That's the *only* way to find what you are looking for.'

'Holy bananapeel,' said Baggywrinkle, shaking his head, 'will we really? I want my eyesight so much.'

'Come on, I'm sure of everything,' she said as she flew up on to his shoulder. 'Let's go inside.'

'But I can't *see* anything.'

'Oh stop *worrying*, you dodo,' she said. 'I'll always be here on your shoulder to peck the direction with my beak. Now come on.'

In the meantime I should describe Timbuctoo a little better for you. She is not half so elegant as the Papillated Ibis, for her neck and beak are smaller. Then again, she is not as silly-looking as the Agate-eyed Albatross because she isn't nearly as fat. Although she's larger than the Bananaquit, she is just as friendly, and you might mistake her for a Bacbakiri Strike Thrush (they are second cousins) except that her tail feathers are not that long. So close your eyes and imagine a bird that isn't too big and isn't too small. Then think of every colour you can and give her a feather of each. Think of all the yellows . . . the colour of butter, and the sun, and lemons and sponge cake, leaves in the autumn and butterscotch sauce . . . and all the greens . . . the colour of mint ice cream, fir trees and grass, spinach and emeralds . . . and all the reds . . . the colour of roses and cherries, bricks and fire and lips and Christmas. Do that for every colour, and then think of Timbuctoo. She is very, very beautiful.

'Five footsteps across the porch, Baggywrinkle,' said Timbuctoo. 'And then reach out to open the screen door. I haven't any hands for such things.'

Baggywrinkle fumbled for the latch and barely managed to get inside without bumping Timbuctoo to the ground.

'Well *done*, Baggywrinkle,' said the Beachcomber as he flipped two pancakes three feet into the air.

Baggywrinkle puffed up with pride. 'Of course, old man,' he said. 'Only ordinary people need eyes.' He swaggered across the room, and ran smack into the piano.

'Patience, my friend, patience. That is what the sea teaches,' said the Beachcomber as he helped Baggywrinkle to his feet. 'You must walk slowly until you learn your way. Now put on these clothes that I've made for you, and let's have some breakfast.'

With a little help from Timbuctoo, Baggywrinkle put on the red shorts and the sailor shirt with the red pockets. The Beachcomber even gave him his own best pair of blue and yellow checked socks to wear with the red wooden shoes. And then the three friends spent a few minutes saying all the right things. The Beachcomber told Baggywrinkle how handsome he looked, and Timbuctoo said she had to admit that the Beachcomber was almost as clever as she was. And the Beachcomber blushed and said it was nothing, really nothing, and the whole time Baggywrinkle felt pleased.

Then they all sat down for their breakfasts – which were all different, because, as the Beachcomber often said, one person's fried hibiscus flower is another person's dried prunes. Timbuctoo nibbled at her sunflower seeds while the Beachcomber had his usual bananas in milk and fried hibiscus flowers. But *you* would have chosen Baggywrinkle's breakfast, for he had the lightest blueberry pancakes you can imagine with a knob of freshly churned butter on each and all the golden honey he wanted to put on top. Every once in a while Baggywrinkle had to be helped. When he couldn't

18

find his orange juice, for instance, Timbuctoo simply pushed it gently with her beak towards his hand. But on the whole, he managed very well.

I wish I could write down all the stories that Timbuctoo told about her travels as they ate, but really, it would fill a whole book by itself. Baggywrinkle listened politely as long as he could, but the taste of the blueberries and the pancakes made him so happy that he suddenly burst into song:

Pancake Song

Banana bake, pancake
Whatever you want
The old man will make

Now I have been told
That sunflower seeds
Served crisp and cold
Some tummies will please

If seeds were my diet
Till age ninety-four
My taste buds would riot
Or I'd be a bore

If you want something yummy
Instead, I'd suggest
To put in your tummy
(It's very diges-

tible) pancakes, pancakes.
Whatever you want
The old man makes!

'Where did you learn to make up a song like that?' asked the Beachcomber after he and Timbuctoo had finished a small round of applause.

'From the first mate on the pirate ship,' said Baggywrinkle.

'How wonderful!' sighed Timbuctoo. 'I shall *have* to take

19

a trip on a pirate ship. Tell me *all* about it, Baggywrinkle. What did the first mate look like?' She put her wings over one eye. 'Did he have a patch?' she asked playfully. 'Do I look like him?'

Baggywrinkle's smile turned sad. 'I don't know, Timbuctoo. I can't see you. I . . . I'm sorry.'

The Beachcomber stood up briskly from the table and started to throw the plates one by one out of the window and on to the sand. Baggywrinkle was so astonished by the thud, thunk, thud of plates as they landed that he completely forgot to stay sad. 'Are you angry?' he asked.

'Of course not. I'm throwing the plates out of the window and on to the sand, where *you* are going to clean them,' answered the Beachcomber. 'Wet sand is the very best for cleaning plates, and Timbuctoo will show you how. Won't you, Timbuctoo? No use frittering away the day. We've got some work to do.'

Baggywrinkle couldn't quite believe the old man, but he went outside with Timbuctoo on his shoulder and knelt in the sand. Then he took a clump of wettish sand as Timbuctoo instructed, rubbed each plate, and brushed off the remaining particles with a cloth. Just to make sure they were really clean, he tried licking his own plate. There wasn't a trace of blueberry or pancake or honey left – just the smooth cool surface of the plate.

'Baggy, tell the Beachcomber what your dream said,' ordered Timbuctoo when the two friends came back into the cottage.

'It said I was going on a long voyage on a perfectly round ship to a river filled with things that are see-through. And at the end of the River of See-Through Things I'll find my eyesight.'

'Well, I'll be—' said the Beachcomber slowly. 'A river filled with things that are see-through, eh? What a lot of treasures it must hold.' He shook his head, almost in a daze at the thought of such a river. 'Well then,' he said, spreading a map on the kitchen table, 'first we need a perfectly round ship, it would seem. Got any ideas, Timbuctoo?'

'Does the sun rise, old man?' answered the beautiful bird as she flew on to the map. 'Now,' she said in her most uppity tone of voice, 'if we are to do this like true World Travellers, we must first maximize all available resources.'

'What does *that* mean?' interrupted Baggywrinkle.

'It means who do we know who has a round ship, you imbecile,' replied Timbuctoo. 'Here we are in the Ivory Coast,' she continued, 'just a few miles east of the city of Sassandra. And across this river, here' (she hopped a few inches on the map) 'lives the Mad Tycoon. And I have it on good account from my contacts in the animal world that the Mad Tycoon has hundreds and hundreds of round ships.' Timbuctoo paused a moment for effect. 'So all we have to do, obviously, is borrow one of his ships and we'll find Baggywrinkle's eyesight in no time!'

'Bumping bananastick!' exclaimed Baggywrinkle, clapping his hands. 'We're going to find a round ship! Three cheers for the Mad Tycoon!'

'Why is he called the MAD Tycoon?' asked the old man.

'Because he's so *madly* cheerful and nice,' said Timbuctoo with a swish of her tail, her beak high in the air. '*I* think it'll be a great adventure to visit the Mad Tycoon. How about you, Baggywrinkle?' she asked sweetly.

'Golly, yes,' said Baggywrinkle, 'it'll really be fun.'

3 The journey begins and Timbuctoo causes some trouble

The three friends set to preparing for the journey to see the Mad Tycoon. While Baggywrinkle sat on the porch and rocked in the old man's rocking chair, the Beachcomber packed two knapsacks. In Baggywrinkle's he packed a picnic and some emergency provisions like peanuts, chocolate bars, and canned tunafish in case they got lost and couldn't find food. In his own knapsack, the Beachcomber packed two sleeping bags, a flashlight and some matches, some gold pieces of money, a book, a game of chequers, and his favourite green umbrella with the holes in it.

Timbuctoo studied the charts and dusty maps to make sure she knew the way on foot, since it is more complicated to travel on earth than in the air. She talked aloud as the Beachcomber worked, explaining that they should walk to the nearest town and ask how to get to the border. At the border, she assured the old man, her contacts could tell her how to find the Mad Tycoon.

'I don't know about all this, Timbuctoo,' interrupted the Beachcomber, shaking his head. 'I don't think we know enough about this Mad Tycoon. We don't even know if he'll lend us a boat. I'm getting too old for hare-brained adventures.'

'You're wise,' said Timbuctoo gently, 'we need you to keep us safe. And think of all the treasures you'll see.' She plucked one of her most beautiful feathers and gave it to the old man. It was the colour of a sunny day when the clouds are high and fluffy in a very blue sky. 'Here is the first treasure,' she said. 'It means we want you with us.'

A large smile shone on the face of the Beachcomber as he stuck the feather in his buttonhole.

'Of course,' said Timbuctoo, 'you can't find treasure without an Expert World Traveller no matter *how* wise you are.'

The Beachcomber laughed and finished the last minute chores. He left some cheese and biscuits on the kitchen table for whoever might come while they were gone, and wrote a note asking that visitors kindly turn off the lamp when they leave.

'Time to be off, Baggywrinkle,' said the Beachcomber cheerfully as he and Timbuctoo came out on the porch.

'You know, I've never been away from the ocean before,' said Baggywrinkle a little sadly as he stood up to go. 'I've been trying to memorize the sound while you were inside.'

'It's always frightening to try something new, isn't it, Baggy?' said the Beachcomber, who just a few minutes before had been doubtful himself! 'But where is your spirit of adventure? We may not succeed, but we'll have a fine time trying. Come on, we're off to find your eyesight!'

With a smile from Baggywrinkle, and one long last look for the Beachcomber at the little cottage by the edge of the sea, the three friends set on their way.

'Now Baggywrinkle,' said Timbuctoo in her uppity tone of voice as they walked along the winding path, 'I think it's important for your education and edification that you know something about this area we are travelling through. And it just so happens I know a *great* deal about it. Are you listening?'

'I suppose so,' said Baggywrinkle. (He was actually thinking about lunch.)

'Right then.' Timbuctoo cleared her voice. 'The principal natural resource of the Ivory Coast is lumbering. The main trading link between Europe and the interior is San Pedro, which deals in palm oil, rubber, coconut, cocoa . . .'

'When's lunch, Beachcomber?' asked Baggywrinkle.

'Don't interrupt,' ordered Timbuctoo. 'Besides, it's only ten o'clock in the morning. Now, perhaps you would like to know *how* palm oil is extracted from the palm tree. First of all . . .'

'But I don't know what extra-acted *means*,' protested Baggywrinkle. 'I don't even know what extra-acted palm trees *look* like. And I don't care, either.'

'Well I never!' said Timbuctoo, ruffling her feathers. 'If you . . .'

'Now, now,' said the Beachcomber, 'it's hard to be interested in something you can't see. Come on, Timbuctoo, we'll take turns describing what we see as we walk.'

There was lots to describe. They were following a narrow path that zigzagged among gigantic ferns and bushes brilliant with trumpet-shaped red hibiscus flowers. Butterflies, the colours of lemons and old lace, flitted among the leaves and huge bees made a gentle, droning song. A few palm trees stood tall and straight with each palm frond reaching for the sun.

The three friends felt very quiet and talked in low tones, partly because the sounds around them were so gentle and partly because the hot sun forced them to walk slowly. Then they came to the edge of the town. Women carrying baskets on their heads sang or called to their friends as they walked along. Families sat outside their red clay houses frying doughnuts on open fires, and tailors sat by the side of the road, sewing at their sewing machines.

Feeling a bit snackish after their walk, the Beachcomber, Baggywrinkle and Timbuctoo all sat down at a picnic table by the side of the road. There were several others sitting at the table and they nodded or smiled at the newcomers. A tall, thin man with smiling eyes and big hands put two generous helpings of bread and butter and two bowls of hot chocolate in front of them. The Beachcomber shared his with Timbuctoo. Baggywrinkle liked the warmth

of the bowl between his hands. He had never felt the river of hot chocolate as it goes down to the tummy, or tasted the crackle of freshly baked bread slathered with melting butter.

'What do you advise us to do, Timbuctoo?' asked the old man as they reached the edge of the town.

'I think we should carry on into the market,' said the bird, 'and ask how to get to the Gold Coast. A train would probably be best, since you two don't know how to fly. I don't mind, of course, but really, you human beings are positively antediluvian about transport.'

'Antedi-what?' asked Baggywrinkle.

'Old-fashioned, to you,' said Timbuctoo. 'Everything you humans devise to move about in is noisy, awkward, smelly, and slow. Except bicycles, perhaps. Birds, on the other hand . . .'

'Now, Timbuctoo, back to your plans,' chided the Beachcomber.

'Well, *you'll* buy the tickets, old man. I don't concern myself with such trivia. Baggywrinkle and I will explore the market.'

The market was a frightening place for Baggywrinkle, since he was bumped and jostled by people crowding between the stalls and tables. When you cannot see, big sudden noises are frightening. Every time someone called out 'make way, make way' or 'look sharp, truck backing up' Baggywrinkle didn't know what to do.

For markets in the Ivory Coast are not like our markets where everything is sold in neat rows and everyone is quiet and no one looks at each other. It's not like that at all in an African market. In fact, it's more like a carnival, or a country fair. For one thing, African markets are outdoors. Long tables are spread with all sorts of curious things – like soaps made of palm oil, drums, and beautiful beads, and snails that shine in the sun. The ground is covered with lemons and papaya fruits and piles of potatoes, oranges, and hot peppers for the buyer to inspect.

'Step lively, Baggywrinkle, you almost pushed over a pyramid of oranges,' whispered Timbuctoo. 'Oops, here comes a man carrying a goat on his back. Move to the side.'

'It's so confusing here,' said Baggywrinkle, feeling frantic.

'Don't worry, the bird whispered, 'you're doing fine. Now walk three steps to the right.'

Baggywrinkle moved forward hesitantly. He could smell fresh pineapple and strange perfumes. 'Why are you whispering, Timbuctoo? And what are those wonderful smells?' he asked.

'I'm whispering because most people don't know that some birds can talk, you dunderhead. Now, all clear for ten yards. March.'

'Hey, curly head,' called one of the market women. 'You taste my papaya, yes? Sweet and good.'

'What's that?' asked Baggywrinkle.

'It's good,' whispered Timbuctoo. 'Say yes.'

The fruit was sweet and warm in Baggywrinkle's mouth. 'That's wonderful!' he exclaimed. 'What can I give you?'

The market woman laughed, waving him away. 'No, no, for your curly hair.'

'You know, Timbuctoo,' said Baggywrinkle as they continued on, 'I don't think she knew I was blind!'

'A puddle coming up, Baggywrinkle. Step to the left,' said Timbuctoo. 'Not too far. You almost hit the chicken crates just then.'

They were standing in front of a chicken stall, and a hundred chickens were cackling and scratching inside their crates. 'Do you think I could hold one of the chickens for a moment?' asked Baggywrinkle.

'Well, I don't know why I should waste my time. . .' said the chicken-keeper. Then he saw Timbuctoo preening her feathers on Baggywrinkle's shoulder. She looked magnificent.

'Where'd you get that bird there, sonny?' the chicken-keeper asked in a suddenly smoother tone of voice. 'You could get a lot of money for her.'

'Sell Timbuctoo! I don't *own* her. She's my friend,' said Baggywrinkle. 'Won't you let me hold a chicken? I've never touched one before.'

'Sure, kid, sure,' said the chicken-keeper quickly. He leaned below the stall counter and whispered to his friend snoozing in the shade. Then he stood up holding a crate, all smiles and politeness. 'Here you go, sonny.'

'It's so soft,' said Baggywrinkle as he took the chicken into his arm. 'And I can feel its heartbeat under the feathers.' Timbuctoo ruffled her feathers with jealousy and stared down at the chicken. Neither of them noticed a small, stocky man with three scars on his forehead sneaking up quietly behind them. It was Konay, the chicken-keeper's friend, and he held a large black bag.

'And the feathers! Are yours all fluffy underneath like this, Timbuctoo?' said Baggywrinkle, stroking her with his face.

'Softer than your bird, isn't it, sonny?' said the chicken-keeper.

'Oh, it *couldn't* be softer than Timbuctoo!' said Baggywrinkle. 'She's the most beautiful bird in the whole world.'

'Is she now?' asked the chicken-keeper greedily. By this time the rascal Konay was right behind the two friends and was slowly lifting the black bag towards Baggywrinkle's shoulder.

'Oh yes,' said Baggywrinkle. 'The Beachcomber says she is a very rare bird.'

The chicken-keeper kept his eyes on Konay as he talked to Baggywrinkle. 'Now, take this rooster,' he said. 'He's a real beauty.'

Timbuctoo had had enough. She was just spreading her wings to fly off when the chicken-keeper winked at Konay. Konay brought the bag down on Timbuctoo, swept her off Baggywrinkle's shoulder, twisted the bag tightly shut and ran into the crowd. The only thing Baggywrinkle heard was one frightened squawk.

'What have you done with Timbuctoo?' cried Baggywrinkle, letting go of the chicken.

'*I* didn't do anything. *You* let my chicken get away,' said the chicken-keeper.

'You just stole Timbuctoo. Tell me where she is,' demanded Baggywrinkle angrily.

'I didn't steal your birdie, sonny. She flew away, that's all. You should have had her on a leash.'

'I'll show *you*,' said Baggywrinkle, his voice shaking with fury. He pushed with all his weight against the towers of chicken crates, and they came tumbling down with a crackling crash. The crates broke open, and all the chickens flew every which way, flapping and squawking with fear. The chicken-keeper shouted to his sister who was selling hot peppers to catch the chickens, and he too went running into the crowd to find Konay and inspect their prize.

At that point Baggywrinkle started to cry. Not the show-offy kind when you make a lot of noise so that someone will pay attention to you. It was the quiet, I-give-up kind. Try as you might, big hot tears run down your cheeks and you feel hot all over. Especially if you're in scorching midday African sun. So Baggywrinkle stood there fighting the tears and feeling frightened and angry and helpless and very sticky and hot all at the same time. He couldn't see anything, he didn't know how to find the Beachcomber, and worst of all, Timbuctoo was stolen. They might sell her, or put her in a cage, or even – horrors – eat her for supper. The thought of that made Baggywrinkle cry all the more.

Then he felt an arm around his shoulder. 'Baggywrinkle, what's the matter?' asked the comforting voice of the Beachcomber. 'Calm down, you're OK. Pretty confusing in the marketplace, isn't it?'

Baggywrinkle tried to talk. He hiccuped instead.

'Where's Timbuctoo ?' asked the old man as he handed him a handkerchief. 'Did she go off and leave you alone ?'

'Th, th, that's the point,' sniffed Baggywrinkle. 'Sh, sh, she's been stolen. The chicken man got her. She's probably de, de, dead by now.'

'Don't be ridiculous,' chuckled the Beachcomber. 'They may *think* they've stolen Timbuctoo, but if I know Timbuctoo, they won't have her for long. Come on, let's see if we can find her.'

The two friends walked quickly up and down the aisles between the tables of the market. The Beachcomber didn't seem very worried.

'Beachcomber, are you *sure* Timbuctoo is all right ?' asked Baggywrinkle.

'I'll bet you a hot chocolate that she's the cause of that crowd,' said the Beachcomber. 'Now let's just go and see.'

As the two friends came up to the edge of the crowd they could hear men shouting at each other.

'You stinking double-crosser,' shouted a short stocky man with three scars on his forehead.

'You putrid little onion,' yelled the taller man shaking his fist.

'You purple-eyed creep,' shrieked the little man.

'Two men yelling,' said the Beachcomber. 'They seem to be angry with each other.'

'It's the chicken-man,' whispered Baggywrinkle. 'It sounds just like him.'

'Good,' said the Beachcomber. 'Timbuctoo must be nearby. If I start to run, Baggywrinkle, you hold on tight and run too.'

The two friends walked slowly around the edge of the crowd while the Beachcomber looked among the tables and the stalls for any signs of Timbuctoo. They could hear the men shouting.

'You slimy little cheater !'

'You mud-slinging swindler!'
'You snivelling liar!'

. . .

'Psssst. Beachcomber. I'm under here.'
'Timbuctoo! Where? I can't see you.'
'Under here. Next to the big basket.'
'Oh Timbuctoo!' exclaimed Baggywrinkle. 'I'm so glad!'
'Shhh,' said the old man. He knelt down under a table piled high with red and green peppers and pulled out a horrible little wire cage. He quickly undid the latch and let Timbuctoo out.

'Well, well,' said Timbuctoo as she shook herself out. '*That's* done. I can explain everything. Getting them to argue was fun. Shall we go?'

'An excellent suggestion,' said the Beachcomber.

So the three friends sneaked away quietly. No one noticed, least of all the two men, because they were too busy shouting at each other. It's hard to notice *anything* when you're shouting.

4 Trouble at the border

With the Beachcomber's hand on one of Baggywrinkle's shoulders, and Timbuctoo sitting on the other, the three friends moved quickly to the edge of the market. They headed for an old run-down stall that had 'Joy to the World' painted in faded red letters over the top and faded painted flowers dotting the sides. Inside the stall sat a man almost as old as the Beachcomber holding eggs up to the sunlight to check that each one was fresh.

'Can you take us to the train right away?' asked the Beachcomber breathlessly.

A fat lumbering man, with a stomach as big as a ten-gallon pickle barrel, pushed himself to his feet with a grunt and grinned at the three breathless friends. Beckoning them to follow, he waddled towards a pick-up truck. Soon they were bumping and jostling down the red dirt road as fast as the clanging old truck would go.

As they drove along, Timbuctoo explained why the men were fighting. Their plan, it seemed, had been to take Timbuctoo to the capital and sell her to the zoo for piles of money. The trick was to convince each of them that the other one wasn't going to share the pay-off.

'Which was easy,' said Timbuctoo, 'for a ventriloquist.'

'Ventrilo-what?' asked Baggywrinkle.

'Timbuctoo is a ventriloquist,' said the Beachcomber.

'I don't understand,' said Baggywrinkle. Then, to his surprise, he heard his own voice saying, 'Oh, now I understand.'

'Hey, what's going on?' he exclaimed. 'That was my voice, but not me talking!'

'*That's* ventriloquism, thick-head,' said Timbuctoo. 'Which means that Konay *thought* he heard the chicken-keeper say, "I'm going to take all the money myself." And the chicken-keeper *thought* he heard Konay say, "I did all the dirty work. Why should he get any money?" *I* was doing the talking, of course, but it set them arguing and I knew I was safe after that.'

'What if the Beachcomber hadn't let you out of the cage?' asked Baggywrinkle sourly. He didn't like being called a thick-head. 'What would you have done then, Timbuctoo?'

'Well, I never,' said Timbuctoo, ruffling her feathers. '*I* can do anything, young man. *I* am a World Traveller.'

Soon the driver pulled the old pick-up truck to a creaky halt just in front of the train station. He turned to look at the three friends squeezed in beside him. 'I'd invite you to lunch, but all I have is three baked potatoes, six boiled eggs and a banana cream pie, and that's barely enough for me,' he said, patting his stomach.

'That's all right,' the Beachcomber reassured him, 'we brought a picnic.'

'All right, then,' said the driver with relief. 'Have a good trip, and watch out for strangers.'

The three friends gathered up their knapsacks, said their thank yous and goodbyes to the driver, and waved the truck on its way. As the dust settled on the red road they plopped themselves down in the shade of a baobab tree.

An hour passed and no train came. Another hour passed. And another. Finally the Beachcomber decided that they'd better see about supper. In West Africa women sit by the station with baskets of boiled eggs, and fruit, and fresh bread. When a train pulls into the station they walk from window to open window, balancing their tower of baskets on their heads as they sell food to the travellers. So the Beachcomber and Baggywrinkle bought their supper and talked with the market women for awhile, and then rejoined Timbuctoo under the baobab tree.

'Beachcomber, do you really think there is a River of See-Through Things?' asked Baggywrinkle. 'And do you really think the Mad Tycoon will lend us one of his ships?'

'I don't know. I hope so,' answered the old man. He leaned back and put his hands behind his head. 'Just think of everything that you would be able to see if you had my eyesight,' he sighed. 'You could see the scratchy, uneven brown of the bark and the smoother brown of the branches over you, and the sunlight sifting through the trees, and all the different greens of the leaves . . .'

'How many different colours of green do you think there are, Beachcomber?' asked Baggywrinkle.

'As many as your imagination can hold,' said the old man.

'That's not true,' said Timbuctoo, who was feeling a bit ignored. 'I have a feather of every colour of green there is, and if you really want to know, all you have to do is count.'

'You must be awfully beautiful,' said Baggywrinkle.

Timbuctoo ruffled her feathers with pleasure and smiled.

'Here comes the train,' announced Baggywrinkle. 'Oh boy, oh boy, I can't wait.'

'The train isn't anywhere in sight,' scoffed Timbuctoo.

'Yes it is,' said Baggywrinkle, 'I can hear it. It's about three miles away.'

The Beachcomber and Timbuctoo looked at each other in astonishment.

'Well, let's see,' said the Beachcomber, looking at his watch, 'that would mean the train would arrive in about four minutes. Let's see how close you are, Baggywrinkle.'

Sure enough, four minutes later even the old man and the beautiful bird could hear the 'doof, doof' of the West African Express coming down the track. The Beachcomber waved his red handkerchief, Baggywrinkle jumped up and down with excitement.

The train came to a sighing stop. The conductor put down

a three-stepped wooden ladder and Baggywrinkle, with Timbuctoo on his shoulder, climbed aboard with the Beachcomber close behind. They plopped their belongings on to two facing benches and then sat down themselves.

'Doof, doof,' went the whistle as the train started up.

There is only one way to describe a West African train, and that is filled to the brim. People sit on all the benches, and some even sit in the aisle. Farmers' potatoes and grains are stacked in pottery jugs in all the corners. Baskets of oranges, eggs, chickens, and fruit fill the middle aisle. Babies cry until their mothers feed them, turkeys cackle, and baby goats bleat.

The noises of the train fade as daylight fades, however, because it is tiring to sit still and do nothing for so long, and most of the travellers were glad to settle down to an early supper of food bought from the market women in the stations. Now many had gone to sleep, curling up on the benches, leaning against each other, or stretching out on the train floor. The Beachcomber had been snoring for quite some time, and Baggywrinkle was drowsy with the day's excitement and the lulling sway of the train.

'I think I'll take a snooze,' he said yawning.

'Yes, you do that,' said Timbuctoo gently, and she nestled into Baggywrinkle's hair. But Timbuctoo couldn't sleep. As the train churned along and the stars came winking out, she thought and thought about what might happen after they crossed the border. For although she would never admit it to her friends, the beautiful bird was worried. She had learned very little in the market about the Mad Tycoon, except that he was very greedy and would do anything to get what he wanted. She didn't even know exactly where to find him, although some snails from the Tana River had told her that he lived very near the border, underground. That didn't sound very easy to find. Timbuctoo didn't feel like a clever World Traveller at all.

Hours later, when most travellers were fast asleep, the

Beachcomber, Baggywrinkle and Timbuctoo sleepily gathered up their knapsacks and got off the train at the border stop. They watched the train turn north, and then started the short walk to the river, where the ferry would take them across.

'The fog is eerie, isn't it?' said Timbuctoo in a hushed voice, as they made their way down the dirt road.

'Mmmmmmm,' agreed the old man.

They walked in tired silence.

Soon they came to a small house on the banks of a dark river. Through the open door, they could see a small man with a face like a weasel asleep at a simple wooden table. A kerosene lamp gave the room a ghostly, flickering light. As the three friends walked in, the man woke with a start.

'Harumph!' he exclaimed, 'you cannot go across.'

'Why in heaven's name not?' asked the startled Beachcomber.

'Everyone crossing the border must have a visa. Rule A43J29X.'

'Nobody told us that in the town,' said the Beachcomber.

'Are you the boy's legal guardian?' asked the customs man immediately.

'Polly want a cracker. Of course you are. Of course you are,' said Timbuctoo in a sing-song voice. 'Polly want a cracker.'

'Why, yes, yes, I am his guardian,' said the Beachcomber.

'Let me see the papers, please. Rule X92J34A.'

'Now look here,' said the Beachcomber. 'I was told in the town that everything was in order and we would be free to go across.' He picked up the Rule Book that was lying on the weasel-faced man's desk. 'This was printed twenty years ago,' he said angrily. 'These rules are out of date.'

'Orders are orders. I do what I'm told,' said the customs man. 'I suggest you leave and come back next week.'

'Polly want to crack him!' said Timbuctoo angrily.

'Come back next week! You must be bananacrazy,'

squeaked Baggywrinkle. 'We have to get across. I need my eyesight. Why, if you . . .'

'Rule J34AX92,' intoned the customs man. 'All inferiors must be quiet. FURTHERMORE: Rule A43J29XX: Everyone must have a visa. LIKEWISE: Rule X92 . . .'

'Come on, you two, let's get out of here,' said the Beachcomber.

Baggywrinkle was sputtering. 'That mealy-mouthed, pigeon-toed bag of warts. He has no right to do that.'

'Unfortunately, my friend, he has the power, and we have not,' sighed the Beachcomber. 'Goodness, this fog is thick. I don't know. Maybe we should go home. I'm too old for this sort of thing.' He was quiet for a moment. 'Let's go down by the water and sort out what we should do next.'

'Beachcomber, look down there. I can see a rowing boat,' said Timbuctoo. 'Come on, you two, hop in. We're going across.'

The wise old Beachcomber hesitated a moment, then looked at Baggywrinkle who was clambering into the boat. Then he got into the boat too.

So there they were, in a boat in the fog in the middle of the night. The Beachcomber was rowing.

'Beachcomber, I'm scared,' said Baggywrinkle.

'Why don't you sing a song?' suggested the old man.

'What about? My songs are always happy.'

'Why don't you try a scared song?'

Baggywrinkle thought a moment, and then he sang softly, to the rhythm of the oars:

Fear Song

We're rowing through fog and through fear
We hope t·at the shore will be near
   Three friends in the night
   There's no need for fright
But we're rowing through fog and through fear.

We're rowing through fog and through fear
We'll be safe just as soon as it clears
   Soon morning will come
   And with it the sun
Which will free us of fog and our fear.

'I like that,' said the Beachcomber softly. 'Will you teach
me the words?'

'Shhhhh,' whispered Baggywrinkle. 'Someone's following
us. Listen.'

The Beachcomber stopped rowing. All three could hear
the churning of a small motorboat – and voices.

'I got all the goods,' came a rough voice about a hundred
yards away. 'And Pina will be there to pick up the load.'

Timbuctoo and the Beachcomber looked at each other
through the fog. Smugglers!

'What kept you so long?' said another hoarse voice in the
dark.

'An old man and his kid trying to go across. Could a been
trouble.'

Baggywrinkle whimpered with fright.

'What's that?' said the rough voice.

'Don't worry,' rasped the hoarse voice, 'it's nothing. But I
wish we could see. Damned fog.'

'Blessed fog,' thought the Beachcomber to himself. He
began to row again as quietly as possible, but instead of
going across the flow of the river towards the other side, he
headed the boat downstream, away from the voices of the
smugglers. Just as they were picking up speed from the push
of the current, the Beachcomber's hand slipped. The flat
side of the left oar smacked against the water and jolted the
Beachcomber's hold on it completely; the oar slid into the
water and floated quickly into the fog.

At that moment, Timbuctoo flew away.

'I'm sure I hear someone,' barked the rough voice.
'What's more, I'm going to find out.'

Baggywrinkle was curled up and shaking with fear. The Beachcomber thought fast. He had to keep Baggywrinkle quiet. He quickly brought in the one remaining oar, bent over, and put his two hands on Baggywrinkle's shoulder to calm the boy. He knew the only chance was if the smugglers neither heard them again, nor saw them – nor bumped into them!

Grug-a-lug-a, grug-a-lug-a. The smugglers' motor boat came nearer and nearer. 'Come on, there's no one out here,' said the hoarse voice impatiently. 'And how about Pina? He's gonna be mad if we keep him waiting.'

'I tell you, I know someone's out here,' hissed the rough voice, 'and Pina's not gonna be too happy if someone's discovered this operation. We gotta get 'em.'

'It's OK, Baggywrinkle,' thought the old man silently. 'Don't cry. Don't make any noise. *Please* don't make any noise.' How the old man wished the boy could see! Just one reassuring smile might make all the difference.

But in fact, the Beachcomber needn't have worried, for Baggywrinkle was now concentrating too hard to cry. He was listening for when the smugglers turned to come back, and listening to hear what they said.

As the old man and the boy listened to the motorboat sputter a large circle around their helpless rowing boat, the Beachcomber squinted and strained his eyes to find Timbuctoo through the dense fog. His muscles were tensed with fear.

Grug-a-lug-a, grug-a-lug-a. The motorboat was coming nearer and nearer. The Beachcomber was sure the smugglers would find them this time. But suddenly Baggywrinkle had an idea. He took off his wooden shoes and heaved them one after another as far as he could away from the rowing boat.

'Hey, hear that? Now do ya believe me?' said the rough voice. 'That's their oars again. Now we'll get 'em.' And the sound of the motorboat turned towards the splash of the wooden shoes – and away from the terrified friends. Baggywrinkle's idea had worked!

Just then, Timbuctoo reappeared. She landed on the bow of the rowing boat and began motioning with her wings. The Beachcomber looked at her hard through the fog, trying to understand what she meant. With her beak, Timbuctoo picked up the rope tied to the bow of the boat and began to fly. Quickly the Beachcomber started to scull again, trying to steer in the direction she was flying. All his muscles were tensed with fear as he sculled through the fog, following Timbuctoo and hoping with all his heart that she knew where she was going.

Grug-a-lug-a, grug-a-lug-a. Grug-a-lug-a.

Suddenly, to his amazement, the Beachcomber realized that the rowing boat was entering a cave!

5 Out of the soup, into the cauldron

It was a narrow cave, like a road of water going through a mountain tunnel. Tiny snails and algae hung on the walls, making an eerie pale glow in the dark. The Beachcomber shivered, and he could not tell if it was from the clammy air, or from relief.

They were safe! Without thinking, the old man reached over and hugged Baggywrinkle, whispering in his ear that the smugglers would not be able to find them now. Just to be sure, he rowed still farther into the cave, while Baggywrinkle whispered that he had heard the smugglers say there would be several more trips across the border that night. The three friends agreed to stay in the cave's shelter until daylight came; now that they were safe, all they could think of was sleep. Looping the boat's rope around a small rock, they climbed on to a flat rock ledge and laid out the sleeping bags. All three fell into a thick and troubled sleep. In his dreams, Baggywrinkle kept rowing towards the round ship they were looking for, only to have a shadowy man spin the boat into space before he could reach it.

After a few hours of restless sleep, Baggywrinkle woke with a start.

Timbuctoo fell off his fuzzy head with a squawk of surprise, and the noise woke the Beachcomber too. They stretched and rubbed the sore places where the rock had been hard, and remembered where they were. (Their adventures the night before seemed more dreamlike than their dreams.)

'Goodness, I would love some fried hibiscus flowers and some bananas in milk,' sighed the Beachcomber. 'Let's see

what's in our food knapsack. I think we left it in the boat.'
He leaned over the rocky ledge to look.

'Timbuctoo,' he said in a choked sort of way, 'did you do
anything to the boat?'

'No, of course not.' She hopped to the rock ledge. The
boat was gone. 'I'll go and look for it,' said Timbuctoo, and
she flew out of the tunnelled cave. Soon she returned with the
gloomy news that the boat was stuck about half a mile
downstream. She had tugged and tugged at the rope at the
bow, but the boat hadn't budged an inch.

'How could the boat have got away?' asked the
Beachcomber.

'*I* don't know,' said Timbuctoo impatiently. 'The
important thing is, how are we going to get out of here?'

'We'll have to crawl along that ledge there,' said the
old man after a long silence, 'and just hope that we don't
fall in.'

'But what about me? I can't see!' protested
Baggywrinkle. 'I'll fall off and drown.'

As calmly as he could, the Beachcomber explained that
the ledge was about two feet wide, wide enough to crawl
along. He, the Beachcomber, would go first, and
Baggywrinkle would follow right behind, with
Timbuctoo on his shoulder to guide him. It was the only
choice they had.

The Beachcomber loaded everything he could into the
remaining knapsack, and then the three prepared to set
off.

'Are you ready, Baggywrinkle?' asked the
Beachcomber gently.

'I, I think so,' answered the boy. 'You won't fly away,
will you, Timbuctoo?'

'No, of course not,' she said kindly.

Baggywrinkle was very, very frightened. Each step he
took made fear go thump in his stomach and he kept
saying 'I'm going to fall in. I'm going to fall in,' over

and over to himself. Actually, he managed very well. First his hand would slide along the rock for a good place to put his weight. Then his knee slid forward too. All the while he kept the right side of his body pushed against the cave wall so that he wouldn't go too near the edge of the water. Reach, glide, rest; reach, glide, rest. As he moved along, Baggywrinkle pressed harder and harder against the wall because he was so frightened of falling in.

'Are we almost there?' he asked the Beachcomber.

'Patience, my friend. We've only just begun. Don't worry. Worry just makes you tired.'

Reach, glide, rest. Reach, glide, rest. Baggywrinkle was pressing harder and harder against the rock wall. Suddenly the wall gave way. Timbuctoo squawked and Baggywrinkle cried out as they fell sideways and down on smooth rock.

'Help!' cried Baggywrinkle in terror.

'Oh shut up,' snapped Timbuctoo. 'I can't see a blinking thing. We must have fallen through a trap door into another cave. Beachcomber?' she said loudly. 'Can you hear us?'

'Yes, yes, very clearly,' said the bewildered Beachcomber. 'But where in the name of good sense are you?'

'I don't know,' answered Timbuctoo, 'but I think we've fallen into another cave. Come back along the ledge and check the wall as you come. Baggy and I will make a noise so you can work out where we are.'

Slowly the Beachcomber inched his way backwards along the ledge, checking the wall with his hands as he went. Suddenly he fell to the side and rolled on to rock, where he stopped with a thunk at something soft.

'Sorry, Baggy. It's me,' said the Beachcomber. He brushed himself off. 'Good heavens, I can't see anything. Are you both all right?'

'Of course,' said Baggywrinkle. 'How did you get in?'

'I'm not sure. It seemed like a trap door. But who on earth would have built a trap door here?'

'Can we get out?' asked Timbuctoo.

The Beachcomber felt the wall with his hands. He could not find a crack anywhere in the smooth cool rock. 'If we can, I don't see how,' he answered.

'Can't see how?' explained Timbuctoo. 'There *has* to be a way.'

'Do you mean that you can't see where you are either, Timbuctoo?' asked Baggywrinkle.

'Of course I can't,' she snapped.

'Well, then,' said Baggywrinkle, 'that calls for a song.'

I Can Find Me

We're not on the land
We're not on the sea
So where on earth
Can we possibly be?

This isn't the jungle
It can't be a cloud
We're not alone
And we're not in a crowd.

We're not in a river
We're not in a tree
Won't somebody tell us
Where I can find me?

'This is not the time for your stupid songs,' snapped Timbuctoo.

The Beachcomber could sense that Timbuctoo was frightened, which was a very rare thing for Timbuctoo. But much as he felt the wall for clues, it was no use. 'If I could see, maybe it would make a difference,' he said. 'But there doesn't seem to be any way back out of here.'

'That's all right,' said Baggywrinkle cheerfully (he was VERY glad to be away from the water). 'We'll just follow this tunnel and see where it goes.'

'Tunnel? How can you tell?' asked Timbuctoo.
'Baggywrinkle, we can't see a thing. It may be dangerous.'

'I'm used to not seeing,' answered Baggywrinkle.
'Come on, I'll lead.'

Since there didn't seem to be any other choice, they
started off, Baggywrinkle first with Timbuctoo on his
shoulder, and the Beachcomber following behind. It
wasn't half so difficult as crawling along the ledge had
been, for the old man and the boy could stand up, and
they could touch the walls to keep their balance without
fear of falling into the water. They had to go very
slowly, however, because it was pitch dark.

None of this seemed to worry Baggywrinkle. He strolled
along humming his song. 'Hey, Beachcomber, there's
a hand rail to hold on to,' he said.

'Why, yes, yes, I've just found it,' answered the
Beachcomber. 'How very, very curious.'

'It's so smooth,' said the boy. 'Doesn't it feel good
under your hand? And you should take your shoes off,
Beachcomber. It feels so cool and smooth under my feet.'

'Your shoes!' exclaimed the old man. 'I'd forgotten
about that. That was awfully clever of you, Baggy.'

Baggywrinkle puffed up with pride and was just about
to burst into a song again when he stopped in his tracks.
'Do you hear what I hear?' he asked.

'No, not a thing,' said the Beachcomber. 'In fact I'd
feel better if we *could* hear some sign of life. This tunnel
was obviously built *by* somebody *for* somebody, and yet
it's so eerie and quiet.'

'No it's not. I hear bells ringing,' said Baggywrinkle.
'Two short rings and then a pause. There they are again.'

'Maybe it's a telephone,' said Timbuctoo.

'Telephones? Underground?' said Baggywrinkle.

'Well, it was just an idea,' said the bird. 'Maybe it's
miners signalling to each other. And they'll show us out
easy as pie.'

'A pie of bananapeels,' muttered Baggywrinkle. He started walking again, this time more slowly. They walked in silence. Minutes passed.

'Wait a minute,' said Baggywrinkle stopping again. 'Now do you hear that? The ringing sound again. And now a buzzing sound too.'

'See? It probably is a mine,' said Timbuctoo. 'Or ... maybe ...'

'Maybe what?' said the Beachcomber.

'Well, maybe this is where the Mad Tycoon lives.

'What do you mean, this is where the Mad Tycoon lives?' said the Beachcomber. 'Don't you *know* where he lives, Timbuctoo? You told me you got directions in the market.'

'I did. The snails in the market told me he lived underground near the border of the Ivory Coast.'

'Hmmph,' said the Beachcomber, 'Some guide you are. I'll go first.'

'No, please, I'll be OK,' said Baggywrinkle. He started off again, wondering why he felt so uneasy when he had felt so cheerful before. 'There's no reason to be scared, is there, Timbuctoo?' he whispered to his friend sitting on his shoulder. He reached his hand up and stroked the beautiful bird.

'I don't think so,' she whispered back. 'But I know one thing. I'll never call you dumb again. It's scary when you can't see anything.'

'Never call me dumb again! Fat chance of that,' he grinned.

Behind them the Beachcomber stumbled. 'Wait for me,' whispered the old man. 'Can you see anything yet, Timbuctoo? I'm beginning to catch glimmers.'

'I don't think so ... well ... yes, yes,' muttered Timbuctoo, tense with concentration as she stared into the darkness. 'The floor looks golden. I think I can see enough to fly now. I'll go and find out what I can.'

Baggywrinkle felt Timbuctoo's wing feathers brush against his ear and the slight pressure of her claws on his shoulder as she took off.

'I wish she hadn't done that,' whispered the Beachcomber as he put his hand on Baggywrinkle's shoulder to guide the boy. 'Something tells me that this time we should have stuck together.'

The old man and the boy continued to walk down the tunnel, which was getting lighter every step they took. The first thing the Beachcomber noticed was that the floor of the tunnel shone with a wonderful golden shine. Then he saw that the hand rail too was golden. Looking ahead, he could see that they were coming to an enormous light-filled cavern. He could hardly believe his eyes.

The cavern was enormous, and it was made of gold. The floor was gold, and the walls were gold. Overhead, a chandelier as big as a cloud glittered with thousands of gold-tipped pieces of glass. Yet trees and gigantic ferns were growing there. A waterfall sparkled and ran over stones in its way until it reached an enormous man-made lake. But most important (it took the Beachcomber's breath away to see them) were *two perfectly round ships* floating in the lake.

'Come on, Baggywrinkle,' whispered the old man. 'I think we've found the right place after all.' He took the boy's hand in his and was just about to walk bravely into the cavern when he saw something that stopped him. In the middle of a raised platform was a very large desk. There was a row of telephones on the desk – thirteen of them – and they were all made of gold. Sitting at the desk with the telephones was a small bald man talking angrily and quickly into three phones at once. He had small beady eyes and a double chin and he wore a gold ring on every one of his fingers. The Beachcomber knew immediately that he didn't like the beady-eyed man at all.

'Beachcomber,' whispered Baggywrinkle impatiently,

'you're forgetting I can't see. What's going on? Can you see Timbuctoo?'

'No,' whispered the Beachcomber. Everywhere he looked were signs that said

DANGER KEEP OUT
NO TRESPASSING ALOUD
THIEVES, SWINDLERS, BURGLARS,
AND ALL UNWANTED PERSONS WILL
BE SORRY THEY CAME. KEEP OUT

BEWARE AND BE GONE

'Surely he'll be kind to lost travellers,' said the Beachcomber. 'Come on, Baggywrinkle, we're going in.'

The two friends walked into the cavern, pretending a great deal of bravery that they did not feel.

6 Meeting with the Mad Tycoon

No sooner had the Beachcomber and Baggywrinkle
walked into the enormous golden cavern when a siren
began to whine and a booming voice called out over
a loudspeaker: 'Attention, please. Invaders at the south
gate. Everyone to their posts immediately. Attention,
invaders at the south gate.'

Before the two terrified friends could even think of
hiding, six guards had surrounded them. 'OK, you two,'
barked the biggest man of all, as two others grabbed them.
Handcuffs clinked shut.

'I beg your pardon,' said the Beachcomber. 'Why are
we being handcuffed? We are NOT invaders. We are
travellers who have lost our way and would be grateful
for your advice.'

'Tell that to the chief,' said one of the men
sarcastically, and pushed the two friends in the direction
of the bald little man.

'Don't push that boy,' said the Beachcomber sharply,
'he's blind.'

'Sorreee, man,' said the guard with a look of respect
for the old man's courage. He directed them across the
cavern to a bench just below the platform. The bench
was made of gold.

'Don't move until you're told to move. Don't talk until
you're told to talk,' said the guard. Then, to the
Beachcomber's astonishment, he lowered his voice and
said, 'If you know what's good for you, flattery will get
you everywhere.' With that, he stepped back three paces
and crossed his arms.

'Now that's some guard,' thought the Beachcomber to himself. 'Don't worry, Baggywrinkle,' he whispered. 'Everything's going to be OK. We're waiting to talk to a funny little man with big ears. He's wearing a T-shirt with palm trees on it, shorts like yours, and yellowy-green shoes, and he looks too silly to be really mean.'

'What's that awful smell?' whispered Baggywrinkle.

'I think he's eating garlic,' answered the old man.

'Yeeech.'

'Mmmmmm. I just wish we knew where Timbuctoo is.'

One of the thirteen gold phones rang. And another one. The bald little man picked them up. 'Hello, Amsterdam? I want three more shipments, at the double ... I don't care what the Greek says, you get those shipments.' He slammed down the phone, and picked up another.

'Jones? Ty here. Foreman tells me that some of the valves on the smasher may be faulty. Check it out.' Slam. He picked up another phone.

'Get Cairo on the line.' Slam. Another phone.

'I want MORE, do you hear me? More, more, more.' Slam.

'Joe, what's the price of diamonds today? Hmmmm. I'll take two bushels. My men will collect. Righto.' Slam.

The little man stood up from the desk, wiped his nose on the back of his hand, and walked down the steps of the platform with both hands deep in his pockets.

'All right you two,' he said squinting at the Beachcomber and Baggywrinkle under bushy eyebrows. 'Thought you were going to steal my gold, didn't you? Well, NOBODY steals gold from the greatest technological genius in the world.'

'Indeed, we had no intention of ...'

'Don't speak until you're spoken to,' barked the garlicky little man. 'What do you mean, you had no intention of stealing my gold? You'd be fools if you didn't want it. Best quality gold in the world, and piles of it, too.' He leaned forward and breathed in a garlicky way into their faces. 'Did you realize that you're looking at the richest genius in the world? Why, I'm so rich I can't stand to look at poor people. That's why I live underground.'

The bald little man picked up a gold dish that had snail-shaped little white things on it. He offered the plate towards the two friends. 'Piece of garlic?' he asked in a suddenly pleasant tone of voice.

'A bit difficult with these, thank you,' said the Beachcomber, holding up his handcuffs. 'Tell me,' he continued, 'are you the Mad Tycoon?'

'Why yes, yes I am,' said the bald little man, puffing up with pride. (It made his double chins even bigger.) He popped some garlic into his own mouth and put the dish down again. 'How nice of you to ask.'

'We've heard so much about you,' said the Beachcomber.

'Oh yeah?' said the Mad Tycoon, suspiciously. 'What have you heard? That I'm a good-for-nothing, double-crossing lout? Or . . .' (he smiled nicely) 'that I'm the greatest technological genius in the world? And the richest?'

'Well, ah, um, actually,' stammered the Beachcomber, 'none of those.'

'I'll tell you what we heard,' piped up Baggywrinkle, 'we heard you were very generous. And that you might lend us one of your ships.'

'Lend you a ship!' screeched the Mad Tycoon. 'Me? Lend one of my precious ships, the pride and joy and technological height of my career? You're fools, or liars. Probably both. Or worse, you're thieves, aren't you??!!'

The Mad Tycoon peered down at the seated Beachcomber with his beady green eyes so that the two men were practically nose to nose. The Beachcomber could barely stand the stink of the bald little man's breath.

52

'You must be very wealthy,' said the Beachcomber, remembering the guard's advice to flatter him.

'Wealthy!' exclaimed the Mad Tycoon, who was jumping up and down. 'Wealthy!' he screeched. 'Why, I'm the richest man in the world, and don't you forget it!'

With that, he took out a little black computer and began to push buttons. 'No, wait,' he said and pushed some more buttons. 'Before I send you to the prisons, I should think up some suitable torture. A deliciously malicious, terrible torture.'

'Torture!' Baggywrinkle blurted out. 'What have we done to deserve torture?'

'You're alive, aren't you?' snapped the Mad Tycoon.

'This is quite a set-up you have here, sir,' the old man said quickly. 'Did you build this place yourself?'

The Mad Tycoon's face turned from a scowl to a smile. 'This?' he said, dismissing it all with a wave of his hand. 'This is nothing compared to what I *can* do. Come, let us have a snack. I have been terribly bored lately, and it will amuse me to tell you about my inventions.'

The old man's mind was racing. One minute this fellow threatened to send them to prison and the next minute he was offering them a snack. No wonder he was called the Mad Tycoon!

But what happened next made the Beachcomber's mind race even more, for suddenly he noticed that a tray filled with delicious food was floating across the cavern towards them. As it settled down on the table next to them, the Beachcomber stared at the tray and then at the Mad Tycoon.

'Nothing, really nothing,' said the Mad Tycoon. 'It was easy once I got round the problem of gravity.' He smiled the smile of the perfect host. 'Won't you have a piece of chocolate cake?'

'What's going on?' asked Baggywrinkle. 'Won't somebody please tell me what's happening? One minute it's off to the dungeons, and now all I can smell is hot chocolate and chocolate cake.'

'It's simple,' said the Mad Tycoon as he handed the boy a plate. 'The point of science is to make magic. The cow jumped over the moon in fairy stories, didn't she? Well, then science made it possible for men to go to the moon. It's as simple as that. The point of science is to make magic. I am a magician. A scientific magician.' The Mad Tycoon popped a piece of garlic in his mouth and smiled broadly at the two bewildered friends. 'Now what do you think of that?'

'What kind of magic do you do?' asked Baggywrinkle.

'Zounds, boy, can't you see? Trays of food float across the room. Trees and ferns sway in the breeze even when there isn't any breeze. I make a lake where there is no lake. Where are your eyes, boy?'

'That's why we're here,' said Baggywrinkle. 'I'm blind.'

'Ah, too bad. Now, as I was saying, would you like to know my best magic?'

'Oh, yes!'

'Please.'

The Mad Tycoon nibbled on another piece of garlic. 'My work is out of this world,' he said and chuckled to himself. Then he scowled. 'But I'm bored. Very, very bored. Do either of you know any physics? Solid state physics?'

'No,' said the Beachcomber.

'Too bad. We could have made up problems for each other. Such a good game. How about chemistry? Or calculus, perhaps?'

'No,' said the Beachcomber, 'I don't know any of those. But I'm not bad at chess.'

'Trite, very trite,' said the Mad Tycoon. 'Oh drat,' he whined, 'why did you have to come and remind me how bored I am? Life is so boring for the richest genius in the world.' An ugly sneer came on his face. 'You didn't come

54

here to play with me, did you,' he snarled. 'You're burglars, aren't you? Come to steal my gold and my secrets, haven't you? Well, you won't get away with it. *Nobody* steals *anything* from the Mad Tycoon, richest genius in the world.'

He began to jump up and down in fury. Baggywrinkle was holding on to the Beachcomber in terror. 'Nobody tricks the greatest technological genius in the world!'

With that he ran to the platform and grabbed a golden megaphone. 'Intercom XS, Intercom XS, page the gaoler and prepare the torture. Intercom XS, do you hear me. Answer me immediately!'

All was silent. Even the waterfall had stopped flowing.

'What's going on?' shrieked the Mad Tycoon, whose face and bald head were red with anger. 'Intercom XS come in immediately.'

Still total silence. Then, to the amazement of the Mad Tycoon, a large booming voice rang out over the intercom. 'All right, Tycoon, we've got you surrounded.'

The Mad Tycoon was so surprised he dropped the megaphone and his computer.

'This is the government's Bureau for Better Business,' continued the large booming voice. 'We're taking you in on charges of smuggling, double-dealing and piracy.'

'You can't do that,' said the Mad Tycoon. 'You haven't any proof! And besides' (he smiled evilly and walked towards the Beachcomber and Baggywrinkle), 'besides, one move to take me in, and you'll never see these two again.'

'Ho, ho, ho,' boomed the voice over the intercom, 'you don't think it's just the three of us, do you? There are two hundred men surrounding this cavern. Touch the old man and the boy, and you'll never get out of here alive.'

'Oh yeah?' sneered the bald little man. He ran to where he had dropped the computer and grabbed it up into his hands. 'You may have two hundred men, mister, but I have

55

the chemical bombs,' he snarled. 'All I have to do is push the right buttons and *none* of us will live. And I'll do it, too.'

But before the Mad Tycoon could do anything dangerous, the Beachcomber ran towards the Mad Tycoon, knocked the computer out of his hand and shoved him to the ground. Then he picked up the computer between his handcuffed hands and hurled it towards the lake.

'What happened?' muttered the dazed Tycoon, who had hit his head when he fell. 'What is going on?'

For a few awful moments, there was total silence. But then, from high in the cavern the flap of wings could be heard, and Baggywrinkle shivered at the sound of a loud, frightened squawk. Moments later a guard appeared, carrying Timbuctoo.

'You're safe!' said the Beachcomber.

'Sorry, boss, he got away,' said the guard. 'But I found this bird in the intercom system. Pina had left his post to check the docks, so no one saw what happened.'

Pina! thought Baggywrinkle to himself. Wasn't that who the smugglers were talking about?

'She is the entire Better Business Bureau and it's army of two hundred men,' explained the Beachcomber. 'She is our friend and was trying to save us. It was a good try, Timbuctoo.'

'You mean *she* figured out the intercom system?' said the astonished Tycoon. '*She* was the loud booming voice?'

'Yes,' said Timbuctoo. 'Most people don't know I can talk.'

'But your voice isn't loud and booming.'

'It can be,' she answered in a loud, booming voice.

Just as if enough peculiar and perplexing things hadn't already happened, just as the three friends were sure that all was lost and that they would never find Baggywrinkle's eyesight – just then, the Mad Tycoon began to laugh. And he laughed, and he laughed, and he laughed. He slapped his knees, held his stomach and rolled on the floor, he was

56

laughing so hard. After a few minutes the three friends themselves couldn't help smiling at the sight and sound of the bald little man rolling on the floor. First Baggywrinkle began to chuckle and then Timbuctoo did too, and even the Beachcomber (who was very worried) had to smile.

'To think,' gasped the Mad Tycoon between bellows and chortles, 'to think that *I* was tricked by a bird!' He burst into fits of laughter again. 'Oh, it's too much. It's just too funny. I haven't had this much fun in years! It's just too much,' he said, wiping his eyes. 'You can leave, guard. We're going to have something to eat.'

'I beg your pardon?' said the Beachcomber.

'Let's have something to eat,' wheezed the Mad Tycoon, 'I can't possibly send you to the dungeons after such a good joke as *that*.' The bald little man stood up, brushed himself off, and pushed some more buttons on his small black computer. The Beachcomber turned to his two friends and gave them both a hug.

7 To the dungeons

Another tray came floating across the cavern, this time
bringing food that smelled and looked so good that the
three friends could hardly believe it was real. The salty
butter smell of fried chicken, the fresh-washed sweetness
of bowls of fruit, the yeasty honeyed fragrance of bread
still steaming from the oven almost made them forget their
troubles.

'Tell me,' said the Mad Tycoon as he chewed at a
drumstick, 'tell me, she-bird, how many languages can you
speak?'

Timbuctoo bristled at being called she-bird, but a warning
look from the Beachcomber convinced her she'd better be
polite.

'I speak all the animal languages except a rare dialect
of dolphin which hasn't yet been translated, and about
fifteen human languages,' she answered. 'In fact I'm a
World Traveller of vast experience. In fact . . .'

'What does a teck-no-logic genius do?' asked
Baggywrinkle. (He wasn't interested in Timbuctoo's
bragging.)

'I invent things, of course,' answered the Mad Tycoon,
passing the gold plate. 'Piece of garlic, anyone?'

'Why?' asked Baggywrinkle as he bit into a big peach
the Beachcomber had handed him.

'Why invent things? To make me the richest man in the
world!' said the bald little man with a toothy grin. 'For
centuries, men have been trying to make lead into gold.
They've tried magic, they've tried philosophy, they've tried

all sorts of hocus-pocus.' The Mad Tycoon jumped to his feet and began pacing back and forth. 'But it took modern know-how, it took science, it took *me* to figure it out.' The Tycoon spun around and looked at the three friends. 'Why I bet you haven't even the foggiest idea how I did it!'

'Did what?' asked Baggywrinkle.

'Turned lead into gold, fool. The riddle of the Middle Ages, and *I* was the one who solved it. A scientific magician, that's me. It was easy, with an atom-smasher.'

'A what-smasher?' asked Baggywrinkle.

'An atom-smasher. It's a scientific fact. If lead is fed into an atom-smasher, it changes into gold.'

The three friends looked blank. Lead into gold?

'It sounds awfully complicated,' said Timbuctoo. 'Does it pay?'

The Mad Tycoon leaned forward and breathed his garlicky breath into the beautiful bird's face.

'You bet it does, she-bird. It's the best quality gold there is, and people pay for that. Creamy, honey-coloured gold.'

'What makes it so good?'

The Mad Tycoon paused for a moment, as though trying to decide how much he should tell them. Finally he said, 'My secret ingredient. Atom-smashed lead turns into gold, all right. But it's boring. No shine, a dull, washed-out yellow. But with my secret ingredient . . .' he kissed his fingers, 'it's magnificent. Princes grovel on the ground for my gold.' He scowled. 'But today I got problems. Big problems.'

The Mad Tycoon yawned suddenly, leaned back in his chair, and began to push buttons on the small black computer that the three friends knew meant trouble.

'What are you doing?' asked Timbuctoo.

'Sending you to the dungeons,' answered the Mad Tycoon. 'You bore me.'

'Sending us to the dungeons!' exclaimed Baggywrinkle. 'You can't do that. You said you couldn't send us there after such a good joke. And we haven't finished lunch. That's going back on your word. That's double-crossing.'

'That's right, runt,' said the Mad Tycoon as he popped another piece of garlic in his mouth and let out a large belch. 'That's life.'

Six large guards came striding into the cavern and stood with their hands on their hips, waiting.

'Now just a moment, sir,' said the Beachcomber, 'isn't there anything we can do to prove to you we had no intention of stealing? Anything at all?'

'Well, maybe there *is* something,' said the Mad Tycoon. He paused for a moment. (The three friends held their breath.) 'No, no, you are of no use to me,' he scoffed as he waved them away. 'I *buy* what I want. Take them to the dungeons, guards, and then to work in the mines.'

Baggywrinkle felt a rough push on his shoulder. As he stumbled forward, he felt he might crash with unhappiness.

'If you pick up any physics in the dungeons, let me know,' called the Mad Tycoon. 'Maybe I'll invite you for lunch.'

Baggywrinkle wheeled around towards the direction of the nasal twang. 'You know what, you bully?' he shouted, 'I used to think there was nothing worse than being blind. Well, I was wrong. It's a lot worse to smell so bad no one wants to be your friend. It's a lots worse not to know *how* to be a friend. It's a lot worse to live underground until you shrivel up and die and have nobody care anyway because you never knew how to be nice. So there.'

'Come on, kid, it won't do any good,' said a guard, and pushed Baggywrinkle on again.

But that guard was wrong. Just as the three friends were about to descend into the earth they heard the Mad Tycoon call out, 'Wait. Guards, bring those prisoners back. On the double.'

'What do you mean I don't know how to be a friend?' said the bald little man as soon as the guards had left.

'Friends aren't mean just to be mean, like you are,'

said Baggywrinkle. 'But you know what made me really angry? It was when you said you could buy what you wanted. Well, I think that's wrong. Everyone in the whole world needs other people, and, and, and, well, if you're a friend you know that. Anyway, that's what I think.'

The Mad Tycoon rocked back and forth on his heels for a moment, staring hard at them.

'It would never work,' he said.

'Try us,' said Baggywrinkle.

'I'd have to tell you more about my business.'

'You can trust us,' said the Beachcomber.

'You'll say it can't be done,' said the Mad Tycoon.

'Sir,' said Timbuctoo, 'we are all three travellers of vast experience, especially me. There is very little you could tell us that we would say couldn't be done.'

'Well then, she-bird, if you're so smart, first I'll ask you a question. Can you talk to spiders?'

'Spiders? Of course.'

'Oh, I don't know,' said the Tycoon, pacing back and forth, 'I don't even know why I even bring it up.'

'Is it dishonest?' asked the Beachcomber.

'Of course not,' said the Mad Tycoon hotly.

'Then try us,' said Timbuctoo.

'Well, then, she-bird, I will. If you can find me twelve large parachutes made of spiders' web, I'll let you go free.'

'Parachutes made of spiders' web?' said the Beachcomber.

'You heard me, old man. That's my offer.' The Mad Tycoon glowered at them. 'If you think I'm nuts you can go to the dungeons right now.'

The three friends sat for a moment in dumbfounded silence. 'Whatever do you want them for?' asked the Beachcomber.

'Couldn't have run my business without them,' answered the Mad Tycoon. 'I hired the leading spider specialist in the world and offered him a million dollars if he could breed spiders that wove huge webs.' He leaned forward and his eyes widened. 'You should have seen those spiders! They were this big!'

He stretched his arms out wide. The Beachcomber shuddered.

'Then what's the problem?' he asked. 'Why do you need us to get you some webs?'

The Mad Tycoon scowled. 'Because they got away. This morning. All hundred and fifty prize spiders. And of course that fool scientist cleared out as soon as he realized it. If I'd caught him he'd be wearing lead-filled sneakers at the bottom of the Tana River.'

The Beachcomber's heart sank. He put his arm around Baggywrinkle's shoulder and gave the boy a hug. Timbuctoo seemed quite cheerful.

'I want to know why you want these parachutes,' she said.

The Mad Tycoon hesitated a moment and then shrugged his shoulders. 'Very well, she-bird, see if you can figure it out, since you think you are so clever. What's the Sun?'

'The Sun? You mean the Sun in the sky?'

'Yeah, that's the one.'

Timbuctoo ruffled her feathers and said in her uppity tone of voice, 'The Sun is a body composed of a high density of gases that gives the earth heat and light.'

'Even *I* know *that*,' scoffed Baggywrinkle.

'Yeah, well, what if I told you there was more to the Sun than that?' said the Mad Tycoon. 'What if I told you that all those gases and heat and light were just a protective covering for another world: the Very Inside of the Sun?'

'Well I'll be,' said the Beachcomber.

'And what if I told you that I go to the Very Inside of the Sun all the time, and that I do business with the Mayor of the Sun?'

'Bumping bananapeel,' said Baggywrinkle.

'What kind of business?' asked the Beachcomber.

'Essence of Yellow, old man. They have a factory, and I need it for my gold.'

'The secret ingredient!' said Baggywrinkle.

'It would be awfully far to fly,' said Timbuctoo, 'even for someone as experienced as me.'

'Do you see those two bubble-shaped ships floating on the fake lake?' asked the Mad Tycoon.

The Beachcomber and Timbuctoo nodded.

'Well, those ships can go to the sun.'

'Bubble-shaped, did you say?' asked Baggywrinkle. 'Does that mean they're round?'

'Yeah, bubble-shaped. What's it to you, runt?'

'Oh, nothing,' said Baggywrinkle.

But the Beachcomber and Timbuctoo knew what he was thinking. Baggywrinkle was thinking of his dream that said he would find the River of See-Through Things – and his eyesight – if he travelled on a round ship!

'How do the ships get to the Very Inside of the Sun without burning to a crisp?' asked the Beachcomber.

'It's really very simple,' said the Mad Tycoon. 'Hydrogen makes the Sun hot. So I figured that if I could neutralize the hydrogen, I could go to the Very Inside of the Sun. And I wanted to go very badly.'

'You mean you make the Sun go out?' asked Baggywrinkle. 'You aren't killing the Sun, are you?'

'No, no,' laughed the Mad Tycoon as he popped another piece of garlic in his mouth. 'I just make a tunnel through the heat layers big enough for a ship. I make a bubble of steamy water.'

'And you discovered the Very Inside of the Sun in a ship like that?' asked the Beachcomber.

'You got it, old man. So, she-bird, the way my space ships slow down for landing on the Sun is by using a parachute.'

'But why Spiders' web?' asked Timbuctoo.

'I'll tell you why,' said the Mad Tycoon. 'It is the

strongest, most flexible material in existence, able to take extreme heat, extreme cold, extreme wet. So that's my deal. I have four parachutes left; twelve more will last me a year and give me time to breed more spiders. If you get me twelve sets of spiders' web parachutes, I'll let you go free. If you cannot get me the parachutes, you can go to the dungeons and work in the mines. That's my offer.' He glowered at them.

Baggywrinkle gulped hard. He wondered if the dungeons were slimy.

'We'll get the webs,' said Timbuctoo. 'No problem?'

'You will?' said the Mad Tycoon.

'We will?' said the Beachcomber.

'Yippee!' said Baggywrinkle.

'That's ducky,' said the Mad Tycoon. 'But just to make sure you don't double-cross me, the runt stays here until you bring me the parachutes.'

'You mean Baggywrinkle? Very well,' answered Timbuctoo. 'I can find the parachutes on my own, so the Beachcomber will stay here too, if he wishes.'
(The Beachcomber nodded.)

'How long will it take you, she-bird?'

'Till noon tomorrow,' she answered.

'Then the deal is twelve parachutes made of spiders' webs by noon tomorrow in exchange for your freedom,' said the Mad Tycoon. 'And if you're not back by noon tomorrow, it's curtains for the runt and the old man.'

The Mad Tycoon pushed some buttons on his small black computer and a guard appeared. 'Show the she-bird the way out,' he ordered.

The beautiful bird turned to go but then turned back towards them. 'By the way,' she said, 'my name is not she-bird. My name is Timbuctoo. Please remember that. Goodbye, Baggywrinkle, goodbye, Beachcomber!'

She was gone.

8 In search of spiders' webs

Timbuctoo was happy to be in the outside world again.
She flew on to the thatched roof of the hut to bask in the
sun. She spread her feathers to air them of the cavern's
clamminess and was just settling into a daydream when
the sound of voices startled her. Children below her were
gathering pebbles in hopes of making the colourful bird
fly. It is not always easy to be beautiful.

Timbuctoo stretched herself free from sleepiness, to the
delight of the children below, and sniffed the air to learn the
direction of the wind. It was a steady breeze from the ocean.

Timbuctoo knew that newly-hatched spiderlings often
use the wind to parachute to other fields before settling down
to weave their webs. Older spiders might make parachutes
too, if they wanted to escape – and it was clear to Timbuctoo
that the Mad Tycoon's spiders had wanted to escape.
By following the wind she might find their parachutes
thrown away on the grass, no longer needed by the spiders,
and very useful to Timbuctoo.

But a pebble zinging by her left wing brought Timbuctoo
out of her thoughts, and she flew quickly to the woods by
the edge of the Tana River. She flew to the highest tree, a
giant baobab.

Then Timbuctoo began to sing. She sang to all the
birds of the forest in the formal way in which birds speak
to each other on important matters. The full beauty of the
song of Timbuctoo would be impossible to capture, for
translation is difficult, and the melody, of course, is lost.

But in order that you understand what happened, here is a glimmering of what she sang:

In the name of your mothers who have brought you nourishment, and in the name of the trees that have protected you, hear my song, O fellow birds. I have need of your help for one who has been a tree, a mighty Iroko, and now is called Baggywrinkle. The same light that gives us food and flight is not given unto this child, and he sees neither the seeds of the earth, nor the corn of the field, nor the clouds of the sky.

But all this can be changed, O most honoured winged ones, and where there was fog shall there be sun for the Iroko child.

Yet is there hope? Yet there is hope if the hateful web of spider that robs us of our flies is gathered. So in the name of my father and mother who were great and honoured among you, in the name of all that brings luck to your nest, in the name of the famines when the lowly spider web robs us of insects more precious than gold, help me now. Follow the breeze, full fifty strong. Come unto the breeze and gather the web.

Then Timbuctoo waited with her breath held. For although she was a confident bird, Timbuctoo was also a young one, and she hadn't had much practise in speaking before a group, let alone asking for something in the formal way of birds. So you can imagine her relief, even amazement, when one by one, then in twos and threes, birds of every size and shape and colour began to fly up from the trees of the forest. Parrots and kingfishers and blue-headed swallows darted and swooped in the air, while larger birds such as the eagles, the herons, and the great flamingoes soared in dignified circles. Soon the sky was filled with a cloud of birds of every kind, chattering and singing hello to each other; it was not often that they had a holiday from nesting and finding food.

Timbuctoo flew among them all, explaining the details of her plan and thanking them for offering help. Then, when all the birds were gathered and all had heard the plan, they formed a long, long line in the air, side by side, about fourteen feet apart. More than two hundred had come, so it was a great and breathtaking sight to see the birds begin their flight in a long, long line together. Timbuctoo herself flew in front, and as she let the wind press against her feathers, and lift her wings, the beautiful bird thought of Baggywrinkle.

The great line of birds flew over the grassy open lands. Soon the jays (who are the natural scouts among birds) began to squawk. Then the great line of birds began their descent, until the field was dotted with their colours.

But the colours of the birds were not the only thing decorating the field that day. Spiders' webs as big as rooms lay upon the grasses like giant blankets of lace. From each corner of the webs, long silken filaments were waving gently in the breeze.

Taking the silken filaments in their beaks, the birds carefully folded the giant webs into packets no bigger than a handkerchief. As the packets were folded, they were placed on two webs left open – a hundred and thirty-six web packets on one and twelve web packets on another. When all the webs were gathered and packed, the web carrying twelve was also wrapped into a bundle that Timbuctoo could carry in her beak. Then twelve of the biggest and strongest birds took the web holding a hundred and thirty-six packets into their beaks and gently lifted into the air. And so it was that a hundred and thirty-six giant webs were gathered for safekeeping by the forest birds of the Tana River, and twelve webs were gathered for the Mad Tycoon.

Back in the cavern, Baggywrinkle was uneasy. Wandering slowly down to the sound of the fake lake (as the Mad Tycoon called it) to feel the cool silkiness of the water on his skin, he sat by the edge with his feet in the water and listened to the nasal twang of the Mad Tycoon.

Maybe it was just his aching feet, thought Baggywrinkle to himself; maybe he just needed a pair of shoes to replace the ones he lost tricking the smugglers.

Soon the Beachcomber joined Baggywrinkle by the fake lake while the Mad Tycoon made business calls. 'I wish you could see the Nimble Thimble,' said the Beachcomber. 'The top half is plexiglass and the bottom half is platinum and diamonds. And it can go anywhere, Baggywrinkle, absolutely anywhere.'

'Beachcomber, when Timbuctoo finds some parachutes and we're free to go, maybe we should just forget about the River of See-Through Things.'

'What do you mean, Baggy? Why?'

'Well, I don't know, I mean, maybe we should just go home and forget the whole thing. I mean, with Timbuctoo on my shoulder I get around pretty well now, and with you around, well . . .'

'You can't rely on us for ever, Baggywrinkle. I'm not always going to be alive, and you never know when Timbuctoo will leave. Besides, there's so much to see. Life is a feast to look at that most people never notice. I want you to see.'

'And I *want* to see,' said Baggywrinkle. 'But everything seems so frightening sometimes.'

'I know,' said the Beachcomber, 'it's hard. But you'll be glad you stuck with it.'

The Mad Tycoon came running up. 'Look, you two,' he said, 'I gotta be going. There's no telling when that birdbrain friend of yours is coming back.'

'She promised to return by noon tomorrow,' said the Beachcomber. 'Timbuctoo always keeps her promises.'

'Promises!' snarled the garlicky little man. 'I have a business to run. Now listen to me. The Mayor of the Sun wants to see me post-haste, so I want you to bring me the parachutes there.'

'Meet you on the Sun! Us?' exclaimed Baggywrinkle. 'You mean leave earth and go to the SUN?'

'Yeah, that's right, runt. No big deal. Just another button to push. You'll sleep most of the way, until a talking computer wakes you. It'll tell you how to work one of the parachutes. You'll need it to go through the hydrogen heat layers.'

'Why waste a parachute on us?' asked the Beachcomber uneasily. 'Why don't we just leave them here for you?'

'That's my business, old man,' said the Mad Tycoon. 'If you want your freedom, you'll have to deliver the spiders' webs to me on the Sun.' He rocked back and forth on his heels as he glared at them with his beady green eyes. 'Of course if you'd rather go to the dungeons and work in the mines, you can do that.'

'How do you know we'll come to the Sun?' said Baggywrinkle. 'How do you know we won't just leave the parachutes here like we promised and then take off.'

'Smart question, runt. Trouble for you is, I've just programmed the Thimble to go to the Sun with you in it, and I've got guards to make sure that you don't change that.'

'But you agreed to give Timbuctoo until noon tomorrow,' said the Beachcomber.

'Them's the breaks, old man,' said the Mad Tycoon. 'See you on the Sun.'

With that, the Mad Tycoon turned on his heels and headed for the second space ship, pushing buttons on his small black computer as he walked. As he shut himself into the ship, the cavern floor between the fake lake and the south gate entrance began to sink, until there was an opening as wide as a road. Water from the fake lake rushed into the opening. Soon a canal of water went from the lake to the water tunnel where the three friends had first escaped the smugglers. The bubble-shaped ship moved through the canal slowly, and finally it disappeared past the south gate entrance.

'Well I'll be—,' muttered the Beachcomber. 'Will wonders never cease?'

At that very moment Timbuctoo was in a rare mood for Timbuctoo; she could not decide what to do. She had the parachutes, and there was no reason why she shouldn't return to the cavern immediately. On the other hand, she hadn't promised to be back until noon tomorrow, and there were no end of exciting things to do.

With her packet of webs around her neck, Timbuctoo played with the wind as she thought over what she would do next. She stretched towards the sun. Then, cradled in a steady current, she glided as far as she could go. Below her some women were harvesting peanuts, first turning over the earth with a hoe and then picking off the nuts from the roots of the peanut plant. One of the women caught sight of Timbuctoo and called to her friend to look at the beautiful bird. Timbuctoo smiled and spread her wings as wide as she could as she flew.

She thought of going to the capital to bask in the sun and catch up with the gossip of the seagulls. And why not, she thought to herself. She could easily be back by noon tomorrow, and the sun on the coast is especially warm. But the thought of sun made Timbuctoo think of her two friends deep in a cavern under the earth, with no possible way to get out until she returned. So Timbuctoo turned southwest towards the little hut on the edge of the Tana River.

'Hello Baggywrinkle, hello Beachcomber,' called Timbuctoo as she flew out of the lift.

The Beachcomber waved to her from across the cavern. 'Have you got the parachutes?'

Timbuctoo landed on Baggywrinkle's shoulder and plopped the packet of spiders' web parachutes on to the Beachcomber's hands. 'Of course I have,' she said. 'I can do anything.'

'That's just grand,' said the Beachcomber, smiling.

71

'You really are awfully clever, Timbuctoo.'

'What's the matter, Baggy?' said the beautiful bird, peering down into the boy's face. 'You're quiet. Aren't you pleased about the parachutes? Tell me how wonderful I am.'

'You're wonderful, Timbuctoo,' said Baggywrinkle dutifully.

'Your travels aren't over yet, Timbuctoo,' said the Beachcomber. 'The Mad Tycoon wants us to meet him on the Sun.'

'Meet him on the SUN!' said Timbuctoo. She sounded a little dazed. She was silent for a moment, then ruffled her feathers and stood up tall. 'Well then,' she said, 'what are we waiting for?'

The three friends piled into the space ship and closed the plexiglass doors behind them. The Beachcomber placed one of the spiders' web parachutes in a small compartment at the top of the ship, while Baggywrinkle bounced on the pillowing that padded the floor.

The old man and the boy fastened their seatbelts, and Baggywrinkle took Timbuctoo on his lap since there wasn't a bird-sized belt. When they were all settled in, the Beachcomber took the control box on to his lap and pulled a button that said:

PULL THIS ONE
TO GO TO THE SUN

Slowly the Nimble Thimble began to move. It crossed the fake lake and passed into the canal just as the Mad Tycoon's ship had done. Soon they were through the dark tunnel, which just a day before they had fallen into by mistake, and were speeding down the Tana River. When they were going too fast to see the trees that edged the riverbanks, the three friends felt the ship tremble, and then, wonder of wonders, the Nimble Thimble lifted into the air like a giant magic bubble and curved higher and higher and higher into the sky and beyond.

72

9 To the Sun

Baggywrinkle sat very still as the Nimble Thimble began its journey to the Sun. His insides felt hollow and his outsides felt numb, and he wondered if he weighed as much as a feather. The Beachcomber and Timbuctoo, on the other hand, were too busy looking out into space to notice how they were feeling. That was understandable, considering what they were looking at. They watched the earth become smaller and smaller until it looked like a multicoloured Christmas ornament hanging in a huge dark room. As the earth passed out of sight, the Beachcomber and Timbuctoo oohed and ahhed every time they passed near a comet, a planet, a glistening shooting star. After a while, however, a quieter feeling crept into them – a feeling of how very, very big was outer space and how very, very small were they themselves. It made the Beachcomber very peaceful. But Timbuctoo was sad in a way that she couldn't explain.

Since Baggywrinkle couldn't see, he didn't feel either peaceful like the Beachcomber, or sad like Timbuctoo. Baggywrinkle felt bored.

'When are we going to get there, Beachcomber?' he asked.

'I'm not really sure,' answered the Beachcomber, who was leaning back with his hands behind his head watching the stars go by. 'The Mad Tycoon told me that the Thimble travels at the speed of light, which means it will probably take nine days to reach the Sun. But the computer can tell us exactly if you like.'

'Nine days! We have to sit here and do nothing for nine days!'

The Beachcomber chuckled. 'Patience, my friend. Remember what the sea teaches. We'll sleep for most of the time, rather like bears when they hibernate, so that we won't need to eat or want to wake up. The computer will wake us just before we reach the Sun's hydrogen layers.'

'I'm bored,' complained Baggywrinkle.

'Then I shall give you a short lecture on inter-planetary flight,' said Timbuctoo in her uppity tone of voice. 'First of all, you must understand that . . .'

'I'm still bored,' interrupted Baggywrinkle. 'Why can't I take off this seatbelt, Beachcomber?'

'Because you'd float up to the ceiling,' answered the old man.

'Bananacool!' exclaimed the boy, and half a moment later, he had unlatched his belt and was floating upwards towards the top of the Nimble Thimble. He bounced gently against the glass.

'Baggywrinkle, I told you not to do that,' said the old man.

'No you didn't. Boy, do I feel strange!' Baggywrinkle did a somersault in the air in slow motion. 'It feels as if I don't weigh a thing! Hey Timbuctoo, look at me!'

'What you fail to realize,' she said dryly, 'is that you were holding me for a reason. I too find myself on the ceiling.'

Baggywrinkle laughed and then he began to sing:

The Somersault Space Ship Song

Round and round and round we go
From under my head to the top of my toe.
Some questions to buy, no answers to spend,
Don't know where I am, or when it will end.

Round and round and round we go
But where is up? Which way do I grow?
I drink from my plate; I eat from my cup.
The moon is now down, and the river is up!

Round and round and round we go,
Confusing, bamboozling since fast is now slow.
So how will I know if ever we're there,
If there is no when, and there is no where?

As he sang, Baggywrinkle floated down to the ground,
pushed off with his toes and soon found himself on the
ceiling again, this time upside down. He did somersaults
in the air and discovered that by pushing off from the
side of the ship he could fly.

'It's magic, Beachcomber, it must be magic,' he exclaimed.

The old man smiled. 'In a way. You could call it scientific
magic, as the Mad Tycoon does. But actually, it's gravity.'

'Oh yes, I remember,' said Baggywrinkle, and wondered
what gravity meant.

After one or two times of bumping his head, since he
couldn't see when he was coming to a wall, Baggywrinkle
was tired and wanted to be back in his seat again with the
seatbelt safely fastened. Finally all three friends were
settled down. The Beachcomber set the controls so that the
computer would wake them at the right time, and they fell
into a deep, peaceful sleep.

For eight days and eight nights the three friends slept
and dreamt. The Beachcomber dreamt of his little cottage
by the edge of the sea and of trees with golden leaves.
Timbuctoo dreamt of a shining white horse with a mane
pure as snow who told her wonderful stories of far-off
lakes and mountains, and of people who never quarrelled.
And Baggywrinkle? The dreams of Baggywrinkle were so
wonderful that, try as he might, he could not remember any
of them. But when he woke up, he felt courageous and bold
and ready to face anything to find the River of
See-Through Things.

Baggywrinkle was the first to wake up after their
eight-day sleep. He heard a voice say:

'This is the computer talking. Please wake up. Only 23 minutes
until the Nimble Thimble enters the hydrogen layers. Are you

ready for instructions? Type yes or no. I repeat: Please wake up.
Only 20 minutes until the Nimble Thimble enters the hydrogen
layers. Are you ready for instructions? Type yes or no.'

Baggywrinkle fumbled for the old man who he knew
was asleep beside him. 'Beachcomber, wake up,' he said,
shaking the old man. 'The Nimble Thimble is talking to
us.'

The Beachcomber sat up and listened.

'This is the computer talking. Please wake up.

Only 17 minutes until the Nimble Thimble enters
the hydrogen layers. Are you ready for instructions?
Type yes or no.'

Quickly the old man typed yes on the typewriter keys
that were on the control box.

'Good. Check that a spiders' web parachute is in place
and then type READY.'

The Beachcomber typed READY, since he had taken
care of the parachute before take-off.

'VERY GOOD. Only 10 minutes until the Nimble Thimble
enters the hydrogen layers. At that time, the Nimble Thimble will
shoot out enormous amounts of liquid oxygen which is very, very
cold. The hydrogen of the Sun plus the oxygen of the Nimble
Thimble will make water. As a result you will be travelling
through an enormous cloud of steamy water. Do you
understand? Type yes or no.'

'Wait a minute, wait a minute,' said Baggywrinkle. 'I'm
all mixed up.'

'The Sun is made of lots of hydrogen, right?' said the
Beachcomber.

'Right,' said Baggywrinkle.

'And the Nimble Thimble is carrying a lot of very cold
oxygen which it can shoot out all around itself, right?'

'Right.'

'Hydrogen plus oxygen makes water, remember?
The Mad Tycoon explained that to you.'

76

'It makes water? Out of thin air?'

'Wise up, dunderhead,' said Timbuctoo. 'We haven't much time.'

Baggywrinkle ignored her. Are we sort of digging a tunnel through the heat of the Sun, except we're using water instead of shovels?' he asked.

'Yes,' said the Beachcomber. 'That's right.' He typed READY.

'This is the computer talking. Only 5 minutes until the Nimble Thimble enters the hydrogen layers. Please be sure belts are fastened.'

Baggywrinkle's heart was thumping hard. 'We're almost there,' he whispered, 'almost to the Very Inside of the Sun. And then the Mad Tycoon will let us borrow the Nimble Thimble, and then we'll find the River of See-Through Things, won't we? Do you think the Mayor of the Sun will know where it is, the river, I mean?'

'I hope so,' said the old man.

'And then I'll find my eyesight, won't I? You'll explain everything when we're in the hydrogen layers, won't you, Beachcomber?'

'I promise,' said the Beachcomber.

'Here we go,' said Timbuctoo, her voice singing with excitement. 'Look at the gases swirling around. Oh Beachcomber!'

The three friends heard a loud hissing sound, like steam from a volcano' The glass on the Thimble clouded, and then they couldn't see anything except billowing white steam, as though they had run into a huge white cloud. The ship began to bump and jiggle, and the three friends held on to their seats and to each other.

'Everything is so white,' said the Beachcomber.

'Is it as scary as night fog?' asked Baggywrinkle.

'Not at all,' said Timbuctoo. 'It's like flying through a cloud in heaven.'

'Is that what's making us bump?'

'Yes,' said the old man.

'But the white is turning into colours!' said Timbuctoo. 'What's happening, Beachcomber?'

All of a sudden the three travellers felt as though they were inside a see-through balloon sailing into a sunset or a rainbow. First Baggywrinkle began to laugh at the crisp crackle of green tickling his face. Then Timbuctoo felt the marshy wetness of misty blue. The Beachcomber felt the cool smoothness of marble grey on his cheeks.

As the rubbery heat of orange oozed into the pyjama-softness of fuzzy pink, the three friends realized a great secret in the rainbow layer of the Sun. They learned that there are hundreds of colours in the world; all kinds of yellows, and all kinds of reds, and all kinds of blues. They learned that all these colours aren't just for seeing, but can be touched and understood. Every colour has a story to tell, and every story is different.

The secret made the friends themselves feel very, very beautiful.

Just then the travellers heard a great flapping sound as the spider's web parachute opened up, and they felt a great splashing flash of yellow. Then everything went thump.

The Nimble Thimble had landed on the Very Inside of the Sun.

10 The very inside of the Sun

The Beachcomber undid his seatbelt and stood up
slowly, for his legs were wobbly from the trip. He opened
the latch of the ship, and soft warm air that smelled
faintly of honey streamed into the Nimble Thimble. The
sunlight was steady and golden and made the leaves
shimmer on the trees.

The first thing the old man noticed was that the Nimble
Thimble rested side by side with the Mad Tycoon's other
space ship. Both were in a grassy 'bowl' that looked as
though it was made by a giant pressing his thumb against
the ground.

'I think we're going to like it on the Sun,' said the
Beachcomber. 'But I wonder who lives here. Do you think
they'll be human beings?'

'Birds, I'll bet,' said Timbuctoo.

'You're awfully quiet, Baggywrinkle,' said the old man
as he helped the boy off the Nimble Thimble. 'Are you
all right?'

'Of course I'm all right,' answered the boy. 'But,
well, something happened to me. I could really feel those
colours when we went through that last patch just before
landing. Or maybe I saw them even. I'm not sure.'

'You mean you can see?' demanded Timbuctoo.

'No, no, not the way I should,' said Baggywrinkle.
'But I think ... I ... know what we're looking for now.'

The Beachcomber didn't say a thing. He just took hold
of Baggywrinkle's hand.

The three friends walked up to the rim of the grassy
bowl. Stretched out below them were miles and miles of

fields, every field a different colour. Pink, purple, violet, red, orange, yellow and gold. From where the three friends stood, the fields on the Sun looked like a giant patchwork quilt. Far in the distance across the patchwork fields was a city. Actually, it looked more like giant golden beehives, all built on one hill. That was all. No cars, no roads, or aeroplanes, or people. Just golden giant beehives.

'That must be where we're going,' reasoned the Beachcomber as he stared at the dreamlike city. 'If the Mad Tycoon's here, that's where we'll find him.' He pointed to a path that led down the hill and across the fields to the city. 'Have you got the parachutes, Timbuctoo?'

'Does the moon shine, old man? I can fly ahead if you like and see what I can find out.'

'No, let's stay together this time,' the Beachcomber decided. 'Baggywrinkle needs you to peck the direction with your beak.'

So the three friends started down the path, with Timbuctoo and the Beachcomber describing everything they saw to Baggywrinkle. Enormous flowers, as big as Baggywrinkle himself, were growing everywhere. There were fire-coloured flowers shaped like trumpets, and strawberry-coloured flowers shaped like strawberries. There were roses as big as the Beachcomber, and daffodils, daisies, and tulips, too. There were flowers as pink as a kitten's tongue, and lacy, star-shaped ones that were bluer than the sky. Some of the flowers were as big as drums and were strong enough to be sat on. Others looked like golden ponies' tails swishing in the wind.

'Look at *those* flowers, Beachcomber,' said Timbuctoo. 'That's the yellowest yellow I ever saw.'

'Better than your feathers?' teased Beachcomber.

'Of course not,' snapped Timbuctoo. 'In fact, even the

flowers of Holland are more beautiful than *these*.'

'Timbuctoo, why do you *always* have to be such a know-it-all?' complained Baggywrinkle. 'I'd give anything to be able to see any flower.'

'What's that flying toward us, Timbuctoo?' said the Beachcomber.

'It sounds like buzzing,' said Baggywrinkle.

Timbuctoo squinted at the dots in the sky.

'It looks like a battalion of giant bees,' she said. 'I hope I'm wrong.'

But the Beachcomber soon knew that she was right: he could see the bees' stingers shining in the light like swords.

'Come on,' ordered the old man, 'we'd better hide.'

The old man pushed Baggywrinkle underneath a gigantic daffodil, pulled it down over the boy and told him to hold on. The Beachcomber had barely hidden under one himself when he heard the giant bees circling high overhead. Their buzzing sounded like chain saws readying to slice a tree into slivers.

Baggywrinkle crouched inside the flower, holding the tips of the daffodil petals to the ground. He was very squashed in, even inside such an enormous flower and, to make it worse, he was sitting on a sharp stone.

'This is crazy,' muttered the boy. 'Why should those bees hurt us?'

Timbuctoo was having a worse time of it; the pollen of the daffodil she was hiding under was tickling her beak. She couldn't stand it any longer. She sneezed so hard that she blew herself right out from under the flower and into the open air. The bees saw her, of course. They flew down at once, buzzing louder and louder and louder. Timbuctoo was surrounded by enormous fuzzy black and yellow bees four times as large as she. One of the bees pushed aside the other flowers with his stinger to find the old man and the boy.

'Don't sting, don't sting,' howled Baggywrinkle.

The Beachcomber held up his hands. 'We come as friends. Have mercy, we beg you.'

Timbuctoo was sneezing and trembling with fear at the same time.

'Why are you so frightened?' asked one of the smaller bees.

'We've come to help you,' said another, 'to save you the long walk across the Fields of Rays.'

'You should not assume we are enemies,' added a third bee.

'Come, climb on our backs,' said the second bee, 'and we shall take you to Hive-Est. There you can meet our Mayor.'

'We're going to fly on your backs?' asked Baggywrinkle.

The Beachcomber turned to Baggywrinkle, surprised at the delight in the boy's voice. 'Won't you be scared, Baggywrinkle?'

'Of course. Have you ever heard of the River of See-Through Things?' he asked the bees.

'You may ask the Mayor. She has the Great Maps,' answered a bee.

'*I've* heard of it,' said the smallest bee. 'But the flight is too long for someone as young as me.'

'You mean it's here? It's really here on the Sun?' asked Baggywrinkle.

'Quiet, beeling,' ordered the older bee. 'It will be better if the Mayor explains,' she said to the three friends. 'Will you come with us now?'

When both the old man and the boy were astride like horseback riders (Timbuctoo preferred to fly herself), the bees took off from the hillside.

'Hold tight,' called out one of the bees. 'You can't hurt us.'

Baggywrinkle dug his hands and knees into the fuzzy

spongy fur of the bee. To his surprise he wasn't at all scared. The air was warm, and he liked the feel of the wind on his face and flapping through his shirt.

As they flew, the bees explained about the Fields of Rays. 'Most sunlight comes from the hydrogen layers surrounding the Very Inside,' explained the bee Baggywrinkle was riding, 'and does not need any attention from Hive-Est. Special kinds of rays, however – one-of-a-kind, rarely seen, and experimental rays – have to be grown in the Fields. You can see them after a storm, when each shaft of light seems like a river of honey streaming down from the clouds.'

'Oh, I want to see it all so much!' said Baggywrinkle.

'And then there are the multicoloured rays of light that you see when you hold a prism up to the sun. We grow those here, too. And rainbows, of course.'

'You mean rainbows are made of sunlight?' asked Baggywrinkle.

'Of course. You went through the rainbow layer before landing,' said the bee. 'That's where we test the rays grown here. Light of different lengths turns different colours. A very short ray of light is red, for instance. That field over there. Longer ones turn purple.'

'Where are you taking us?' asked Baggywrinkle as the bees started in slow spirals downward.

'Into the golden city of Hive-Est, city of golden beehives,' replied the bee. 'There you will meet with our Mayor, Her Beeing-Est.'

'Is she nice? Does she sting?'

'She is a just leader. And she knows everything,' answered the bee. 'Hold on, now. We're coming in for a landing.'

No sooner had Baggywrinkle's feet touched ground when Timbuctoo was on his shoulder chattering as fast as she could. 'Baggywrinkle, you wouldn't believe it even if you *could* see. This is the most beautiful city I've ever seen. In all my travels I've never seen streets paved with gold before.'

'Are we in Hive-Est?' asked Baggywrinkle.

'Of course, stupid. Can't you smell the lemon trees and the oranges? Everything's clean and there are vines dripping with grapes and flowers. All the buildings are round and coloured white or golden. The bees say that most of the beehives are factories, but they don't look like factories.'

The Beachcomber put his hand on Baggywrinkles' shoulder. 'How'd you like flying like that, Baggy? Beats the Nimble Thimble, doesn't it?'

Baggywrinkle smiled at his friends and nodded. 'Where's the Mayor?' he asked. 'I have to ask her if she knows where to find the River of See-Through Things.'

'Of course, Baggywrinkle,' said the old man, 'we can go right away. We just thought you'd like to know what we're seeing. But come on, the bees are waiting to take us to her.'

With bees leading the way, the friends started walking through the streets of Hive-Est. They were beautiful streets, paved in gold as Timbuctoo said, with white and gold walls on either side hung with ivy and other deep green vines. Often the walls had doors so that Timbuctoo and the Beachcomber could see into beautiful courtyards filled with lemon and organge trees, fountains, green grass, and gardens filled with enormous flowers. Sometimes the streets widened for a fountain with flowers all around where buzzing bees were gathering pollen. In fact there were so many bees that Baggywrinkle and the Beachcomber soon tired of dodging through the crowds as they walked uphill and down through narrow winding streets. One of the bees finally noticed their difficulties, and soon they were flying down the streets on bee backs, feeling like visiting kings.

The Beachcomber leaned forward so that the bee he

was riding could hear him above the buzzing of the crowds. 'Is there any reason for having so many gardens? Why do you bother to grow flowers on the sides of the beehives too? Are they there to be beautiful?'

'Sun's alive, no, old human one,' answered the bee. 'We need several tons of pollen every day to make the honey which is the main ingredient in Essence of Yellow. Pollen comes from flowers. It seems only natural to have the raw ingredients near the factories.'

'But why have everything so crowded?' asked the old man. 'Why did you build Hive-Est on this hill when you could have built it on the plains?'

'By building up instead of out, we make best use of the space we have,' explained the bee. 'We need the fields to grow the rays and the flowers.'

'Here we are at the gardens of the Mayor,' said the bee that Baggywrinkle was riding. 'You may address her as Her Beeing-Est.'

The three friends walked shyly into the courtyard. They knew at once which bee was the Mayor. She was larger than the other bees, and her fur was especially shiny and soft. She had large brown eyes that were kind and no-nonsense at the same time. Baggywrinkle said that she smelled of lemonade.

'You're late, aren't you,' said the Mayor. 'Never mind, never mind. A butterscotch, anyone?'

'Yes, please,' said Baggywrinkle.

'Good. Now, I haven't got all day,' said the Mayor as she handed Baggywrinkle a bagful of sweets. 'State your case.'

'We've come to give the Mad Tycoon his webs,' said Timbuctoo, 'which I was clever enough . . .'

'I'm looking for the River of See-Through Things,' interrupted Baggywrinkle.

'That's beside the point,' answered the Mayor.

'What do you mean?' asked the Beachcomber.

'The Mad Tycoon says you *stole* the Nimble Thimble. *He* says you should be arrested immediately.'

'He's lying,' said Baggywrinkle angrily.

'I should have known,' sighed the old man. 'I should have known.'

'He's lying,' repeated Baggywrinkle.

A tear rolled down Timbuctoo's face and landed on Baggywrinkle's shoulder. 'That rotten egg,' she whispered. 'That dirty rotten egg. Now Baggy will never have his eyesight.'

'That smelly double-crosser,' said Baggywrinkle. 'We didn't steal the Nimble Thimble, Your Beeing-Est, I promise. He lent it to us. We've lived up to our part of the deal, and now he's got to live up to his. It's not fair.'

'There must be some way we can prove we're innocent,' said the old man.

'Of course there is,' said the Mayor. 'Just show me some proof that he lent you the Nimble Thimble. State your case.'

'But we haven't any proof,' said Baggywrinkle. 'We thought we could trust him.'

'Trust the Mad Tycoon? You should be more careful whom you trust.'

'If you don't like him, why are you sticking up for him?' asked Baggywrinkle.

'My job has nothing to do with liking or disliking. My job is to be just. If you've stolen the Mad Tycoon's ship ...'

Just then the Mad Tycoon came storming into the courtyard belching garlicky belches. His stomach jiggled up and down.

'There they are! Those are the thieves!' said the Mad Tycoon as he pointed to the three friends. 'Those are the ones I told you about. Put them in jail at once!'

'Good afternoon, Tycoon,' said the Mayor. 'Thank you for coming so quickly to identify the accused. Their guilt has not been proven, however. There will have to be a trial.'

'But we'll lose if there's a trial,' protested Timbuctoo. 'We haven't any proof.'

'Exactly,' screeched the bald little man. 'Of course they're guilty! Everyone saw them land! Everyone knows the Nimble Thimble belongs to me!' He whirled towards some bees and stared into their faces. 'Doesn't the Nimble Thimble belong to the Great Tycoon?'

'Yes, sir.'

'We never said it didn't,' said Baggywrinkle angrily.

'Didn't you see those three evil strangers come in for a landing in my ship?' asked the Tycoon.

'Yes, sir.'

'Of course we did. You *said* we could,' said Baggywrinkle even more angrily.

The Mad Tycoon turned back towards the Mayor, ignoring Baggywrinkle. 'The bees even told me that these thieves hid under the flowers when they saw the bees coming. In cahoots with the flowers! They're guilty, I tell you. Put them in jail.'

'Do try to be reasonable, Tycoon,' said the Mayor. 'I admit the evidence is against them. But they still must have a trial.'

The Tycoon was jumping up and down with rage. 'No, no, no,' he shouted. 'Put them in jail. If you value my business you'll put them in jail!'

'Hey, Tycoon, look what I've got!'

Everyone in the courtyard looked up towards the sound of the voice. There on the courtyard wall, safely out of the Mad Tycoon's reach, was Timbuctoo, swinging the packet of spiders' web parachutes around her neck.

88

'Hey, Tycoon,' she repeated, 'how about these parachutes?'

'You got them!' exclaimed the Tycoon. He rushed towards the bird. 'Give them to me. At once.'

'Certainly not,' said Timbuctoo as she flew to the opposite wall of the courtyard. 'If you won't give us our freedom as you promised, we're not going to give you the parachutes.'

'Give them to me,' shouted the fat little man.

'If you break your promise, we don't have to keep ours.'

'You, you, you,' spluttered the Mad Tycoon. 'Give me those. I'm the only one who needs them.' He ran at Timbuctoo, who just flew to the opposite wall of the courtyard.

'Hey, what are you going to do now?' she taunted.

Suddenly the Tycoon realized that he was only making things bad for himself. He turned to the Mayor with a calm, evil grin.

'Your Beeing-Est,' he said, 'the crimes of these thieves are even worse than I thought. Not only did they steal the Nimble Thimble: they stole my small supply of parachutes too, my precious supply of parachutes. I myself gathered the spiders' webs you see round her neck and sewed them together, piece by piece, all by myself.'

The Tycoon rocked back and forth on his heels. 'Without parachutes I cannot come to the Sun. And you know what that means, Mayor. No more business, Your Beeing-Est. Gone, finished. No more gold ... So if you know what's good for you, you'll make that she-bird hand them over.'

'He's a double-crossing liar,' cried Baggywrinkle. 'Timbuctoo got those parachutes because he asked us to. He's lying, Your Beeing-Est. He's lying.'

'Shut up, runt,' shouted the Tycoon. 'Those parachutes belong to me.'

'HE'S LYIIIIIING!' shouted Baggywrinkle.

'Nothing will be decided,' said the Mayor, 'by shouting.'

'Give me those parachutes,' screeched the Mad Tycoon. 'I demand justice. If you ...'

'Tycoon,' interrupted the Mayor, 'there is no possible way for me to reason with Timbuctoo while you are shouting and carrying on. And you, Baggywrinkle, will keep your voice down.' The Mayor looked sternly at them all.

'Perhaps we can settle this out of court,' she continued. 'If the alleged thieves agree to give back the Nimble Thimble, will you drop charges against them, Tycoon?'

'Never. I want them in jail. I demand justice.'

'As you know, Tycoon, the minimum jail sentence is a hundred years,' said the Mayor. 'Surely if they are willing to give back the Thimble ... Surely there is room for mercy.'

'Justice!' bellowed the Tycoon. 'They stole my ship! A hundred years is too short. I want them in jail for ever.'

'But we didn't steal it,' protested Baggywrinkle.

'Prove it,' sneered the Tycoon.

'I must have some time alone with the prisoners,' said Her Beeing-Est. 'If you'll be good enough to leave ...'

'I don't want to leave,' said the fat little man sulkily. 'And where's my supply of garlic, anyway?'

The Mayor sighed. 'Please do as I ask.'

A gleam came into the eyes of the Mad Tycoon. 'Well, then, I won't leave unless you let me go into the Essence of Yellow Factory.'

'The Factory?' said the surprised Mayor. 'Only the workers are allowed in there. You know that. I've told you that before.'

'I won't leave you alone unless you let me see inside the factory,' repeated the Tycoon, stamping his foot.

The Mayor sighed again and shook her head. She turned to one of the other bees. 'Take the Tycoon to the factory.

Let him have a good look around. Tell the bee in charge that it is in thanks for all that he has done for us.'

The Mad Tycoon had a horrible grin on his face as he left the courtyard. At the door he turned to the three friends. 'I never thought you'd get this far,' he sneered. 'But you'll never get any further.' He laughed. 'Have a nice time in prison. I hope you rot.'

He was gone.

11 The plot thickens and boils

For a few moments after the Mad Tycoon left not a word was said. Timbuctoo flew back on to Baggywrinkle's shoulder, and the Beachcomber put his arm around the boy. Finally Baggywrinkle spoke.

'Do we have to go to prison right away?' he asked.

The Mayor laughed kindly. 'Of course not. You haven't been proven guilty yet.'

'What if we *are* proven guilty?' asked the Beachcomber.

'By Sun law, you'll go to jail for a hundred years,' answered the bee.

'I'd never travel again,' cried Timbuctoo.

'I'd never see my cottage.'

'I'd never have my eyesight,' wailed Baggywrinkle.

'Well, it won't do any good to think about it now,' said the Mayor briskly. 'The trial hasn't even begun. You may win, you know.'

'But we haven't any PROOF,' they all said at once.

'I know, I know. It's terribly difficult,' said the Mayor. 'Justice is a sticky business, I've always said.'

A bee flew into the courtyard from a side door carrying a tray with toast and tea with honey on his back. Her Beeing-Est thanked the bee and poured tea for the three travellers.

'You need the Mad Tycoon's business, don't you?' asked Timbuctoo.

'In a way,' said the Mayor. 'It's a curious story. Would you like to hear it?'

'Yes, please.'

'Well then. Once upon a time, a long time ago, when the Sun crossed paths with the Moon more often, all who lived on the Sun lived in peace, and the bees and the flowers worked together to make Essence of Yellow. But the flowers became unhappy working all the time, and so they went on strike. The story of the strike and how we reached the Great Compromise would fill a whole book and I shall not tell it now. Anyway, by the time the strike was over, our Essence of Yellow was almost all used up. The skies were grey day after day, and the world was becoming colder.'

'So what happened?' asked Baggywrinkle.

'We all had to work four times as hard as before, and the factories had to be rebuilt.'

'What factories?' asked the Beachcomber.

'The Factory of Sunrays, the Laboratory of Light Research, the Essence of Yellow Factory – all of them. We needed bigger and better factories – and quickly, or the Universe would die.'

'Wow.'

'What did you do?'

'We started to build the city of Hive-Est. The problem was the bricks we used. Bee-bricks had worked before. But those were the smaller factories before the Great Compromise. Now that the factories had to be so much larger, bee-bricks were not good enough. The walls were crumbling as fast as we built them. And we were running out of Essence of Yellow.'

'What would happen if you did?'

'The hydrogen layers make heat, not light. Without the Essence of Yellow there would be no light on Earth, and everything there would die.

'Just as we were sure that all was lost,' continued the Mayor, 'the Mad Tycoon arrived on the Sun. It was like magic. He said that if we would give him Essence of

Yellow, he could make the strongest, most beautiful gold in the world. Half the gold he would give to us to build our city, and half he would keep himself.'

'Then you had to trust him too, didn't you?' said Baggywrinkle.

'It worked for you,' said the Beachcomber sadly. 'No wonder you have to be nice to him. The Mad Tycoon is saving the Sun.'

'He *saved* the Sun,' corrected the Mayor. 'Hive-Est is now built, and we no longer need the gold. Now we sell Essence of Yellow to the Tycoon only as thanks for what he did. As soon as the contract runs out, we won't sell him another ounce of Essence of Yellow.'

'The Mayor paused to choose her words carefully. 'The Mad Tycoon is not loved in the city of Hive-Est. Unfortunately for you, everyone on the Sun has seen him come and go, and everyone knows that the Nimble Thimble belongs to him. No matter what we think of him, justice is justice. Unless you can show proof that he did lend you the ship, you will probably end up doing hard labour for a hundred years. Now, why don't you tell me your side of the story? Baggywrinkle, you start.'

In fits and starts the three friends told their story: how Baggywrinkle was carved into a mast and became a boy, how he was blind, and what his dream said; how they travelled from Ivory Coast to Gold Coast to find the Mad Tycoon; about the smugglers and finding the cave; how Timbuctoo found the parachutes and how they flew to the Sun.

'Why ever did the Mad Tycoon want you to meet him on the Sun?' asked the Mayor.

'So he could double-cross us,' said Baggywrinkle. 'He's got the parachutes he needs and then lets you put us in jail to get rid of us. He's a smelly, double-crossing liar.'

'Hush,' said the Mayor. 'You've got to prove that. I

can't help you find the River of See-Through Things if you're in jail. Are you sure you haven't any proof that your story is true?'

Just then a messenger bee came flying into the courtyard, buzzing loudly. 'You must come quickly, Your Beeing-Est. The Mad Tycoon has gone crazy. He is climbing the machinery in the Essence of Yellow Factory. He's shouting that he's taken over the Sun. He has a gun!'

'I'll have to come myself. Climb on these bees,' said the Mayor to the three friends as she rose into the air. 'You too, Timbuctoo.'

With the messenger bee buzzing the crowds out of their way, they raced through the streets of Hive-Est. They flew so fast that the flowers, the lemon trees, and the courtyards were only a blur.

'Thank the Sun you're here, Mayor,' buzzed the gatekeeper bee as he opened the golden door of the factory. 'I knew he shouldn't have been let in.'

The Beachcomber and Timbuctoo could hardly believe their eyes. They were in a huge room as big as a circus tent, but with ceilings twice as high. Platforms and metal pots hung from the ceiling like trapezes and swings made for giants. But most amazing of all were the bees, thousands and thousands of bees. They were everywhere – on the walls, on the platforms, on the ceilings – the air was thick with them. Thousands of bees were carrying daffodil petals, lemons, buckets of honey, and piles of tin cans to be melted in the huge pots, pots as big as rooms, that hung from the ceiling. Thousands more bees poured the melted ingredients on to platforms below. Still others raked the platforms, throwing down lumps to be melted. On the ground below the platforms was a black pot as big as a house. On it was written in large golden letters:

ESSENCE OF YELLOW

A flaming furnace belched fire beneath the pot. The

factory was sweltering hot from the flames, and the buzzing of the working bees roared in Baggywrinkle's ears like ten trains passing by.

The Beachcomber put his hand on Baggywrinkle's shoulder. He had spotted the Mad Tycoon. Somehow the Mad Tycoon had climbed up on to the platforms, although, with no ladders, it was hard to see how. He was jumping from platform to platform, waving a gun in the air and shouting things they could not hear over the roaring buzz of the worker bees.

'Why doesn't anyone stop him?' shouted the Beachcomber to the bee who had brought them in.

'Working bees, the drones, don't stop for anything. Drones don't notice anything except their work.'

'What if he falls?' shouted Timbuctoo.

'Is it boiling?' asked the Beachcomber, pointing to the huge pot of Essence of Yellow.

'It's hotter than fire on earth.'

They watched the Mad Tycoon waving his gun in the air as he shouted words they could barely hear over the roaring buzz of the drones.

Meanwhile, the Mayor had flown to the control room and signalled the Head Bees to keep the drones as quiet as possible. Now the words of the Mad Tycoon could be heard easily as the drones continued to rake and pile and pour and mix.

'I'm bigger and better and stronger and richer,' shouted the Mad Tycoon. 'Do you hear me, drones? Down with the Mayor!' he yelled. 'I'll rule the universe. Essence of Yellow belongs to me. Make more, I say!'

He leapt to a platform that was piled high with lemons.

'Tycoon, can you hear me?' shouted the Mayor. 'Put down your gun, PLEASE, so we can fly in and rescue you. There is not much time, Tycoon, DO YOU HEAR ME, there is not much time.'

'No, ma'am, you ol' honey-talking sweetie bee,' yelled

the Mad Tycoon. 'I'm too smart for you. *I'll* rule the universe now.'

He danced about on the platform, waving his gun in the air like a madman.

'No honey without Essence of Yellow,' he sang.

'No gold without Essence of Yellow,' he
  bellowed.

   'No sunlight without Essence of Yellow,' he
    howled.

    'No Essence of Yellow without me,' he
     crowed.

    'NO NOTHING WITHOUT ME!!!!'

'Tycoon, the platforms are due to tilt any second.' shouted the Mayor. 'You're in danger. Put down your gun so we can fly in to rescue you.'

'You're wrong, you're wrong, you're deliciously wrong!' shouted the Mad Tycoon. 'Make more, you buzzers, make more!' And he began again to dance about on the platform of lemons.

'They're doing what I say, you see
So the factory belongs to me.
Make more!
They're doing what I say, you see,
So the factory belongs to me.
Make more! Make more! Make more!'

The Mad Tycoon leapt to the platform of honey. But no sooner had the fat little man, with his fat stomach and his fat head, jumped onto the platform when the right weight was reached and the platform began to tilt. All the sticky, gooey, runny, sunny, gleaming, golden honey began to flow into the enormous pot of bubbling, boiling Essence of Yellow.

'Hooray for me!' yelled the Tycoon at the top of the platform. 'Wheeeee,' he laughed as he started to slide. But then he saw the pot of boiling essence. From where

he was, slipping and sliding down the platform of honey,
it looked a gigantic sea of lemon pudding.

But it wasn't.

And the Mad Tycoon suddenly realized it wasn't.

'Help!' he cried, trying to grab on to the oozy, squeezy
honey. But it was too late.

AIEEEEEEEE
               E
              E
             E
            E
           I
          I
         E
        I
       E
      H
     H
    H He shrieked as he fell,
                              fell,
                                fell

into the bubbling, boiling pot. Splat.

The Mad Tycoon was dead and melted in one half-
second.

The Mayor flew over to join the three friends. 'There
was nothing I could do,' she said. 'By the time he let go
of the gun, it was too late.'

They were all silent.

'Mayor, Mayor, something has gone wrong.' It was the
Head Drone, and he was looking very worried.

'Yes, Head Drone?'

'This batch of Essence of Yellow is covered with an
oily green slick. We don't understand. Something extra
must have been added.'

'Yes, yes, I understand,' said the Mayor a little sadly.
'You'd better just throw this batch away.'

12 Why Baggywrinkle leaves his friends behind

The three friends didn't do much of anything those next few days after the Tycoon died. The Beachcomber was 'tired to the bones', as he said, and Timbuctoo wanted to explore Hive Est. Even Baggywrinkle didn't mind waiting around – at first.

It was a pleasant few days filled with storytelling, and picnics, and walks through the gardens and streets of Hive-Est. Yet there is nothing much to tell, for it is a queer truth that happy times are quickly told, and difficult times take enough words to fill a book.

Early on the third day, however, things changed. The Mayor had proclaimed a holiday in memory of the Mad Tycoon, and everyone was excited. Everyone except Baggywrinkle, that is. Feeling grumpy, he was kicking pebbles around after breakfast when Timbuctoo flew on to his shoulder and began to chatter.

'Guess what, Baggy, there's going to be a parade, and *we* are the honoured guests. Isn't that super? Don't you think my feathers will make the flowers jealous?'

'How about the River of See-Through Things?' said Baggywrinkle. 'I thought we'd leave today to find the River.'

'Oh you and your silly River,' snapped Timbuctoo. 'can't you think of something *else* for a while? Think about me.'

'Come along, you two,' called the Mayor from across the courtyard.

'What is Baggywrinkle upset about?' asked the Beachcomber. 'Do you know, Timbuctoo?'

'I haven't the foggiest idea,' sniffed Timbuctoo.

'Oh well, he'll cheer up,' said the Mayor. 'Let's go.'

Out in the streets everything was noise and confusion, for the parade was about to begin. There were huge floats decked with growing flowers and bee marshals were buzzing about telling everyone to line up. The flowers were singing rounds, the sunlight was specially bright, and everyone was happy that it was a holiday.

Except for Baggywrinkle. As usual, Timbuctoo had flown off to explore. So she wasn't there to explain what was happening. And the Beachcomber wasn't paying attention to him at all. There were so many bees that none of them noticed Baggywrinkle, and the boy was sure that one of the bees was going to sting him, anyway.

As soon as Baggywrinkle bumped into a wall, he sat down and leaned against it, hoping he wouldn't get stung. His bare feet hurt.

'Hello, human child. It's me, the beeling. Remember me? I'm one of the bees who found you in the flowers.'

'I think I remember your voice,' said Baggywrinkle. 'Yes, I'm sure I do. I *am* glad to hear you. Nobody cares about me, and I don't want to be here at all, and ...'

'Don't want to be here?' asked the beeling. 'Where do you want to be?'

'At the River of See-Through Things,' said Baggywrinkle. 'But stupid Timbuctoo wants to be in this stupid parade, and I don't know where to find it.'

'You mean the River?' asked the beeling. 'Well, *I've* found out where the River of See-Through Things is.'

'Have you?' squealed Baggywrinkle. 'Will you take us there?'

'Of course. Let's go right away.'

'Bananacool! But first I'll have to get my friends.'

'You don't need *them*,' scoffed the beeling. 'It'll be an adventure. You're not scared to go by yourself, are you?'

100

'I suppose not,' said Baggywrinkle. 'I mean, of course not. I'll show them. Let's go at once. While they're not looking.'

'Climb on my back,' said the beeling. 'I'm strong enough to carry you until we're outside the city. Then you'll have to walk.'

Before you could say – think twice before you jump – Baggywrinkle and the beeling were flying out of Hive-Est and into the Fields of Rays.

'My wings hurt,' complained the beeling as they wound their way along the path in the hot sunlight.

'So do my feet,' said Baggywrinkle. 'We must have been gone hours and hours.'

'Can you see the River of See-Through Things yet?' asked the beeling.

'Of course not,' said Baggywrinkle. 'I can't see anything. You're the one who's supposed to know where we are.'

'But I do,' said the beeling. 'We're in the Fields of Rays, between a patch of purple and a patch of blue. But when are we going to get to the River?'

'I *told* you, I *don't know.*'

'I'm sorry,' said the beeling. 'I forgot.'

'Let's rest a moment,' said Baggywrinkle wiping his forehead. He plopped himself down, and rubbed his feet. They were very sore.

'Baggywrinkle, I'm thirsty. Can I have a drink of water?'

'Good idea. I'd like one too. Where's the water?'

'Haven't you got any?' asked the beeling.

'No, I haven't,' said Baggywrinkle crossly. 'Come on, let's go.' He stood up and started walking again.

'But the older bees *always* carry water when we go through the Fields of Rays,' wailed the beeling as he flew to catch up.

I'm NOT a BEE,' snapped Baggywrinkle. 'You should
have worked *that* out by now. I'm just as thirsty and
frightened as you are.'

The beeling began to cry.

'I'm sorry,' said Baggywrinkle, 'I didn't mean to be
cross. Come on, where are you? I'll carry you for a while.
The path is easy enough.'

The boy took the fuzzy beeling into his arms, lifted him
up on to his shoulders and continued walking. For a while
the little beeling sniffled, but the tears had stopped, and
soon Baggywrinkle realized that the beeling had fallen
asleep. He was buzzing gently.

So Baggywrinkle walked carefully, trying to keep in a
straight line so that he would stay on the path and not
bump into the patches of blue and purple. He walked and he
walked and he walked. And tired though he was,
Baggywrinkle kept on walking, hoping with all his heart
that he was going in the direction of the River of
See-Through Things.

13 The River of See-Through Things

After looking through all the gardens and courtyards
of Hive-Est for Baggywrinkle, a search party led by
the Beachcomber and the Mayor set out in the Nimble
Thimble across the Fields of Rays, with bees flying out
in all directions from the city, like waves when a pebble
hits a pond. They finally found the boy asleep in a patch
of golden rays, with the little beeling curled up beside him.
Timbuctoo plopped down on his curly hair and tickled his
ear with her beak.

'What's that sitting on my head?' mumbled
Baggywrinkle as he woke.

'It's us, Baggy. We've been looking everywhere for you,'
said the Beachcomber. He gave Baggywrinkle a hug.

'Oh Beachcomber, I'm so glad you're here,' said
Baggywrinkle. 'Running away hurt my feet too much, and
I didn't know where we were.'

'Here's some water,' said the Beachcomber kindly. 'It
must have been frightening.'

Baggywrinkle gulped the water and gave some to the
little beeling.

'You, beeling, must come to court tomorrow,' said the
Mayor. 'You should not have led Baggywrinkle out into
the Fields of Rays.'

'No, no, don't get angry with him,' said Baggywrinkle.
'It was my fault, too.'

'All right, just this once,' said the Mayor. 'I think the
beeling's learned his lesson.'

'Now can we go to the River of See-Through Things?'
asked Baggywrinkle.

'Yes, Baggywrinkle,' said the Mayor, 'we can go there now.'

'We can? Is it nearby?' asked Baggywrinkle.

'Of course it is,' said the Mayor. 'The Sun makes the day see-through, doesn't it? And the sky becomes see-through, and raindrops, and teardrops, and diamonds and lemonade. And rivers, Baggywrinkle, sunshine makes rivers become see-through, too. Doesn't it?'

'Now I understand,' said Baggywrinkle. 'There's a special River of See-Through Things on the Sun because sunlight makes the night and everything else see-through.'

'Do you see the V in the Prismatic Mountains to the north, Beachcomber? Sail the Nimble Thimble towards the V until you come to a deep lake, and land on the water. I'll meet you at the silver gates at the far end of the lake.'

Her Beeing-Est flew off. Baggywrinkle, the Beachcomber and Timbuctoo waved goodbye to the bees who had helped them, and piled into the Nimble Thimble. Soon they were flying low over the Fields of Rays away from Hive-Est towards the V in the mountains.

'You know, Beachcomber, I learned something from the little beeling,' said Baggywrinkle. 'He kept asking me questions that I couldn't answer. It's hard to be the one who always has to give the answers.'

'Come on, pinhead,' said Timbuctoo. 'You ask the Beachcomber questions all the time.'

'I know,' said Baggywrinkle, 'that's the point. It made me see that the Beachcomber's probably just as scared as I am sometimes.'

'That sun must have gone to your head,' said Timbuctoo.

'Maybe so,' said Baggywrinkle happily. 'But we're going to the River of See-Through Things, and that calls for a song.'

The See-Through Song

Up, backwards, and forwards,
Down, inside, and out.
Able to look every which way
Is what it's all about,
To be see-through.

If I were totally see-through,
Would I be totally me?
I'd be able to find what I looked for,
But I don't know what that would be.

If you were totally see-through
Would we be totally we?
If I tried to tell you a secret,
Could you keep it so no one could see?

If the world were totally see-through
Would the world be a good place to be?
How would we find one another?
And wouldn't you bump into me?

Up, backwards, and forwards,
Down, inside, and out,
Able to look every which way
Is what it's all about,
To be see-through.

Timbuctoo was the first to see the deep, deep lake, and the
Beachcomber landed carefully on the water. Neither the
bird nor the old man, however, could see any silver gates.
Neither said a word. But Baggywrinkle pointed in the
direction of the mountains and said, 'Go that way. I can
hear the Mayor buzzing.'

They met the Mayor halfway across the lake. She flew
into the Thimble.

'We're only just in time she said, 'and we'll have to
hurry or it may get to late. Tnight is the full moon, and
Baggywrinkle must be at the Source of the River by the
time the moon rises.'

The silver gates were in sight, shining so brilliantly that the Beachcomber and Timbuctoo could hardly bear to look. Pillars as tall as trees stood on each side of the gate, and at the top of each pillar was a perfect diamond egg as big as a child that spun around on itself. Engraved on the gate itself was a creature such as they had never seen before; it had eyes, horns, and golden wings.

'What is it?' whispered the Beachcomber.

'The symbol of Erikefon-Est,' said the Mayor quietly. 'She who appears and reveals. The River belongs to her. Read the riddle to Baggywrinkle. He should guess it easily.'

Slowly the Beachcomber read the riddle written on the gate.

Daylight is like this river
The water is wide and true,
If you name the name of this riddle,
The gate will see you through.

What is the name of my River?

'We're here,' said Baggywrinkle, his voice shaking. 'We finally found it. The River of See-Through Things.'

As soon as Baggywrinkle said its name, the two diamond eggs spun even faster than before, and the gates began to open. Slowly, as though the whole Sun was being moved, the gates opened wide.

The Nimble Thimble sped along the River. Honey and balloons and lemonade and windows and lollipops were floating in the water. Dandelion fluff, and dew, and mica made the water sparkle and glitter like stars. There were even bowls of jelly and glasses of lemonade floating by.

'Faster, Beachcomber, faster. We haven't much time,' urged Her Beeing-Est. 'Erikefon-Est is easily angered.'

'Look, Beachcomber, look at the amber beads, and the prisms, and the bubbles: oh look at the beautiful bubbles!' said Timbuctoo.

'Will you tell me everything I have to do?' Baggywrinkle asked Her Beeing-Est.

'I promise,' she answered. 'But you'll have to do it all by yourself.'

'What do you mean?' he asked.

'There is an old, old lullaby that all the children on the Sun hear from their grandparents before they go to sleep at night, It goes like this:

If you can climb as high as the sky,
You will catch two stars, as they shoot by,
And if you have friends who helped you get there,
Those stars will become two new eyes rare.'

'I have to climb as high as the sky?' asked Baggywrinkle.

'If you want your eyesight.'

'But how?'

'Don't worry,' said Her Beeing-Est. 'You'll see.'

Suddenly the Nimble Thimble went BUMP. Then it shivered, which made all four travellers shiver too. The Thimble stopped moving completely'

'Are we there?' asked Baggywrinkle.

Timbuctoo and the Beachcomber looked around. Facing them was a grove of willow trees planted in a half-circle around the most beautiful waterfall they ever could have dreamed of. The waterfall shimmered with thousands of raindrops and teardrops and diamonds and dew. A light wind made all the thousands of droplets fall in gentle spirals into the River itself in shimmering, shining see-through veils of water.

'Yes,' said the Beachcomber. 'It's the Source of the River.'

'We're here!' cried Timbuctoo. 'We're really and truly here! I'm so happy I think I'll cry.'

'Don't be a bunglehead,' said Baggywrinkle happily. 'We haven't much time. How do I climb as high as the sky, Your Beeing-Est?'

'You'll have to climb the highest willow tree,' she buzzed softly. 'By yourself.'

'Climb a tree by myself!' exclaimed Baggywrinkle. 'But I'm blind.'

'Yes,' she said.

'All by myself? Without any help? Without Timbuctoo on my shoulder?'

'Yes,' she said.

'But that's not high enough to catch a star!'

'Every month,' explained the Mayor, 'on the night of the full moon, the Source is even more splendid than usual. (Hail to the name of Erikefon-Est.) Just as the sunlight dims and the full moon rises, the raindrops and teardrops and diamonds and dew harden into stars and are blown into the night by one gust of wind. By the goodness of Erikefon-Est, that is how all the shooting stars that have fallen from the sky are replaced . . .'

'You'll have to hurry,' added the Mayor, looking at the sky. 'It's not long till moonrise and you have to climb the highest willow.'

'I can't,' said Baggywrinkle. 'I'll fall, I know I will. I'm too blind to climb a tree.'

No one siad anything. Everyone waited.

Silence.

Silence.

Finally Baggywrinkle spoke. 'Beachcomber? Timbuctoo? If you would show me to the willow tree, I'd be very grateful.'

Timbuctoo and the Beachcomber stood at the foot of the tree and hoisted Baggywrinkle on to the first branch.

'Good luck,' whispered the beautiful bird.

'Have patience, my friend, and go slowly,' said the Beachcomber. 'You'll make it. Just remember what the sea teaches.'

Baggywrinkle reached up and took hold of a branch. Then he slid his foot up the trunk till he found the next branch and lifted his weight on to it. The bark felt rough

under his hands. Then he slid his foot up the trunk again, found a branch, started to climb – and bumped his head.

'I can't do it,' he said to himself. 'I can't.'

He moved his head slowly to one side and tried again. He didn't hit his head.

'Maybe I can.'

He climbed up another branch, and then another.

'Hurry, Baggywrinkle, hurry,' called Her Beeing-Est. 'The sunlight is dimming.'

But Baggywrinkle couldn't find another branch to climb to. He groped and fumbled and felt all the way around the trunk. He couldn't find a branch.

'Now I really can't,' he thought. 'It's just too hard. I'll fall, I know I will.'

He thought of his friends down below, hoping and holding their breath. 'I've got to,' he thought to himself. 'They believe in me. I must. I must.'

Then Baggywrinkle remembered how the pirates used to shin up masts using their hands and knees. He took a deep breath. Gripping the trunk of the tree with his knees he reached with his hands and his arms. Up a few inches. And a few more. Higher and higher and higher Baggywrinkle climbed, until he could feel the willow tree begin to sway.

From down on the ground, Baggywrinkle was out of sight, and the sunlight was fading fast. Just as the full moon appeared, a sudden gust of wind blew through the willow trees; and the raindrops and teardrops and diamonds and dew of the fountain were flung by the wind like glitter into the sky. Moments later, the Beachcomber, and Timbuctoo, and Her Beeing-Est heard a voice call out high, high, above them:

'Blooming bananapeel, I can see!'

Epilogue

Since magic never ends (it is just a little harder to find sometimes) you might like to know that the three friends got home safely after the Mayor of the Sun decreed that the Nimble Thimble would for ever after belong to them.

Back in West Africa, the Beachcomber built a safe place for the Nimble Thimble close to his little cottage by the edge of the sea and then settled down happily looking for treasures. Timbuctoo, who was not one to stay still long, soon set off again on her World Travels. And Baggywrinkle? Baggywrinkle stayed with the Beachcomber. He had lots to discover now that he could see, especially since his eyesight was a very special kind.

But that's another story.

Kevin Crossley-Holland
Sea Stranger, Fire-Brother and
Earth Father 70p

Three stories of Wulf the Saxon boy and Cedd the holy man who
converts him to Christianity in the dark and dangerous years of the
seventh century : Wulf, lying dreaming among the ruins of the
Roman fort, becomes Cedd's first convert after his sea-journey from
Northumbria to the land of the East Saxons ; Wulf's new life of peace
and learning among the monks is envied by his own brother Oswald
– then someone sets fire to the crops the monks have been
growing . . . Wulf makes the dangerous journey to see his old friend
when news comes that Cedd is dying of the plague.

Thomas Rockwell
How to Eat Fried Worms 60p

Billy takes up the bet and launches upon a nightmare feed –
munching away bravely to win that fifty dollars. Creamed worms,
fried worms, boiled worms, worms with peanut butter or horseradish
sauce – he can eat them any way he likes, just as long as he eats them !
When it looks like Billy's winning the bet, Alan and Joe have to try
and stop him – or he'll walk off with their fifty dollars !